A
POEM
FOR
EVERY
WINTER
DAY

EDITED BY ALLIE ESIRI

*Also edited by Allie Esiri
from Macmillan*

A Poem for Every Autumn Day

A Poem for Every Night of the Year

A Poem for Every Day of the Year

Shakespeare for Every Day of the Year

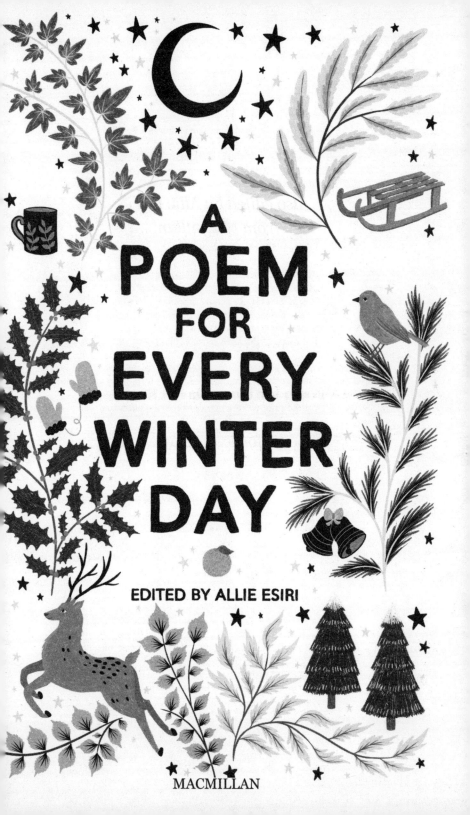

A POEM FOR EVERY WINTER DAY

EDITED BY ALLIE ESIRI

MACMILLAN

Published 2020 by Macmillan Children's Books
an imprint of Pan Macmillan
The Smithson, 6 Briset Street, London EC1M 5NR
EU representative: Macmillan Publishers Ireland Ltd, 1st Floor,
The Liffey Trust Centre, 117–126 Sheriff Street Upper,
Dublin 1, D01 YC43
Associated companies throughout the world
www.panmacmillan.com

ISBN 978-1-5290-4525-3

5 7 9 8 6 4

A CIP catalogue record for this book is available from the British Library.

Printed and bound by CPI Group (UK) Ltd, Croydon CR0 4YY

For Rosie Esiri

Contents

January

ix

February

Introduction

In this anthology *A Poem for Every Winter Day*, the second in a four-part cycle of seasons, you will discover some of the most engaging poems ever to be written about Winter, and the major cultural touchstones and historical landmarks that mark our calendars between December and February.

This wintry collection comes bearing something of an unexpected gift to you, the readers ('tis the season after all). For although the title of the book promises one daily dose of verse, you will, in fact, find that each date is accompanied by two poems, almost all of which have been selected from my previous curated anthologies *A Poem for Every Day of the Year* and *A Poem for Every Night of the Year*.

Each of these poems are prefaced by a short introduction that provide some essential background context — either about the poem's author, style or content — and the occasional anecdotal gem. But this isn't an academic book, and you won't find anything in the way of jargon-heavy analysis and long literary interpretation here. A poem makes its greatest impact when the reader can engage in a tacit dialogue with the writer, without extraneous distraction.

Although day and night can seem almost indistinguishable during winter, these poems are broadly split into those that can motivate and inspire on a damp, chilly morning, and those that invite us to reflect and offer solace in the evening over a cup of camomile tea. This is, all told, the season of guilt-free, idle cosiness, when there are no expectations to venture out and conquer the world, and what better way to while away those hours curled up indoors than to immerse yourself in the myriad worlds created by the words of the great poets.

Not everyone is a fan of winter, of course. Anyone who has trudged back to school or work on a typically drizzly first week of January would probably be inclined to refute T. S. Eliot's famous claim that April is the cruellest month. The nineteenth-century French poet and novelist Victor Hugo meanwhile was rather unambiguous in his views on the season, declaring in his tome *Les Misérables*, 'Winter changes into stone the water of heaven and the heart of man.'

This inextricable association of winter with misery, callousness and hardship is deeply ingrained in our day-to-day language. Words that describe seasonal weather such as icy, gelid, frosty, dark and cold have long been synonymous with passionless apathy at best, inhumanity at worst; there's a reason Shakespeare didn't attempt to compare his lover to a winter's day . . .

But for those of us who aren't called Richard III, winter can be about so much more than discontent. Yes, it's the season of pitch black mornings and darkness that envelops us from early afternoon. But it's also a period in which multiple iridescent lights bathe our streets and our skies, heralding the arrival of the festivities of Christmas, Hanukkah, Diwali and New Year. The grey, dreary days seem a small price to pay when, once in a while, a blanket of snow transforms our usual surroundings into unrecognizable, dreamlike landscapes. It is a time of retreat, inertia and insularity but also for slowing things down, for intimacy and reuniting with families. And while

Winter has always been seen — from Shakespeare to *Game of Thrones* — as an ominous portent of death and evil misdeeds, it is also the season of renewal, fresh starts and love across the world, thanks to the celebrations of New Year and Valentine's Day.

The 150 or so poems that make up this anthology remind us of all there is to cherish in, and glean from, this perhaps most misunderstood season. There are pieces, such as 'Stopping by Woods on a Snowy Evening' by the aptly-named Robert Frost that revel in the joys of nature in winter, and reveal how much vitality exists in the world even when plants die and animals escape into hibernation. Other texts, from Sappho's 'The Moon' to Mary Oliver's 'Some Questions You Might Ask' present and encourage moments of quiet meditation, befitting these less boisterous days. There are also those wonderfully steeped in nostalgia such as the extract from William Wordsworth's 'The Prelude', and there are poems such as Emily Brontë's 'Spellbound' that address the very real, emotional and physical hardships posed by the arduous winter months. Each poem then is like a snowflake, entirely unique.

Some are rarer than others, however. Within these pages there are, of course, old favourites by everyone from William Shakespeare to Robert Burns, Emily Dickinson to Christina Rossetti, Thomas Hardy to Percy Bysshe Shelley, and the bard of the bears, Winnie-the-Pooh (whose acutely insightful 'Tiddely-Pom' arguably captures the quintessence of the season better than any other text). But unlike other anthologies, which are too often deferential towards the established canon, this collection seeks to give a voice to those lesser-known geniuses — the contemporary mavericks, international masters and female doyennes — who have been inexplicably overlooked and unrepresented until now. So alongside Alfred, Lord Tennyson, William Wordsworth and W. H. Auden you will discover Charlotte Mew, Eleanor Farjeon, Mary Oliver, the ancient Greek 'Poetess' Sappho, and other global greats including the Spaniard Federico García Lorca, the Japanese haiku pioneer Issa, the Chinese 'Poet Immortal' Li Bai, and the present-day Jamaican polymath Kei Miller.

Many works included in this anthology, such as the latter's 'Parting Song', may not seem especially wintry at first glance — in fact, Miller's piece makes repeated mention of light blue skies. But winter days are not just about snowmen and ice-skating. There are days, just like any others, filled with the gamut of human emotions, from blissful contentedness to aching longing, as seen in Housman's 'Yonder See the Morning Blink' and Shakespeare's *Romeo and Juliet*.

And there are winter dates that are singular in what they represent, and are commemorated by poems that illuminate the nature or significance of those specific days. It goes without saying that this includes Christmas with a series of poems and carols, New Year's Eve (Burns's 'Auld Lang Syne'), Twelfth Night (Eliot's 'Journey of the Magi') and Valentine's Day (Wendy Cope's 'Valentine). But it also means paying tribute to the likes of Holocaust Memorial Day on 27 January (Niemöller's 'First They Came for the Jews'); Martin Luther King's birthday on 15 January (poems by the great African-American writers Maya Angelou and Langston Hughes); the anniversary of Rosa Parks's heroic bus-based act of civil disobedience on 1 December (pieces by Joseph Coelho and Jan Dean), and even the day on which man first set foot on the South

Pole on 14 December (Derek Mahon's 'Antarctica').

The ability to find a clear sense of unity with the poets seems especially vital for a winter anthology. There will be times, when faced with biting wind and a shroud of interminable darkness, that we may feel lonely and defeated. It's in these moments that we can turn to poems such as 'Dawn' by Ella Wheeler Wilcox that remind us that we're not alone in our experiences, or to the likes of Jackie Kay's 'Promise', Blake's 'Infant Life' and Philip Larkin's 'First Sight' that give us hope that change is just around the corner; although perhaps Shelley put it best in his 'Ode to the West Wind' with his reassuring question, 'If winter comes can spring be far behind?'. Here you'll find everything you need to galvanize your mind or soothe your spirit from every winter until spring comes around again — and a new anthology for that season appears!

Allie Esiri

December

1 December • Joseph Coelho •
Rosa Parks – 1st December 1955
Lillie Mae Bradford – 11th May 1955
Claudette Colvin – 2nd March 1955

On 1 December 1955, an African American woman from Alabama, Rosa Parks, refused to give up her seat in the 'white section' of a segregated bus. She was arrested on charges of civil disobedience, but her actions would become a symbolic, watershed moment for the American civil rights movement. Parks later worked with the National Association for the Advancement of Colored People (known as the NAACP), a group which, to this day, strives to secure equality and rights for African Americans.

Not the first to sit.
Not the first to get arrested.
Not old (she was 42).
Not tired ('Just tired of giving in.').

One of many, unable to sit
with the injustice of years.
A rider on an old road
walked by millions on tired legs.

These riders fought for a seat,
years in the trudging,
of sole-worn protest
walked in frustrated miles
over landscapes of lives.

2

One day became thirteen months;
of continued mapping,
of hitchhiking and car pools
of walking and tattered shoes
because the bus
wasn't going anywhere they planned to go.

While Joseph Coelho places Rosa Parks within the context of centuries of oppression, in this poem, Jan Dean celebrates the individual, heroic act of defiance by a woman who could no longer stomach the complete absurdity and injustice of racial segregation.

she sorts the drawer
knives at the left
forks at the right
spoons in the middle
like neat silver petals
curved inside each other

the queue sorts itself
snaking through the bus
whites at the front
blacks at the back

but people are not knives
not forks
not spoons
their bones are full of stardust
their hearts full of songs
and the sorting on the bus
is just plain wrong

so Rosa says no
and Rosa won't go
to the place for her race

she'll face up to all the fuss
but she's said goodbye
to the back of the bus

'Still I Rise' is a powerful poem in which the speaker declares an intention to transcend the bitter realities of black experience in America. The verses gradually break down and are replaced by a repeated statement of defiance: 'I rise.' The text has moved and inspired generations of readers, not least Angelou herself, who claimed it was her favourite poem from her own body of work.

You may write me down in history
With your bitter, twisted lies,
You may trod me in the very dirt
But still, like dust, I'll rise.

Does my sassiness upset you?
Why are you beset with gloom?
'Cause I walk like I've got oil wells
Pumping in my living room.

Just like moons and like suns,
With the certainty of tides,
Just like hopes springing high,
Still I'll rise.

Did you want to see me broken?
Bowed head and lowered eyes?
Shoulders falling down like teardrops,
Weakened by my soulful cries?

Does my haughtiness offend you?
Don't you take it awful hard
'Cause I laugh like I've got gold mines
Diggin' in my own backyard.

You may shoot me with your words,
You may cut me with your eyes,
You may kill me with your hatefulness,
But still, like air, I'll rise.

Does my sexiness upset you?
Does it come as a surprise
That I dance like I've got diamonds
At the meeting of my thighs?

Out of the huts of history's shame
I rise
Up from a past that's rooted in pain
I rise
I'm a black ocean, leaping and wide,
Welling and swelling I bear in the tide.

Leaving behind nights of terror and fear
I rise
Into a daybreak that's wondrously clear
I rise
Bringing the gifts that my ancestors gave,
I am the dream and the hope of the slave.
I rise
I rise
I rise.

On 2 December 1805, Napoleon fought the Battle of Austerlitz against a Russian and Austrian army, triumphing over them in what is now remembered as his greatest victory. But in this humorous piece, the Czech poet (and scientist) Miroslav Holub wittily reveals that even ruthless emperors cannot conquer time . . . or capture the attention of distracted school children!

Children, when was
Napoleon Bonaparte born,
asks teacher.

A thousand years ago, the children say.
A hundred years ago, the children say.
Last year, the children say.
No one knows.

Children, what did
Napoleon Bonaparte do,
asks teacher.

Won a war, the children say.
Lost a war, the children say.
No one knows.

8

Our butcher had a dog
called Napoleon,
says Frantisek.
The butcher used to beat him and the dog died
of hunger
a year ago.

And all the children are now sorry
for Napoleon.

In the Winter of 1812, Napoleon's army was advancing into Russia. This ill-advised campaign during the bitterly cold Russian Winter eventually led to the destruction of the French army. This short poem is framed as a speech from Napoleon to his troops during this campaign, but it might as well be a soliloquy. For Napoleon, the Russian landscape only reflects his inner emptiness and isolation.

'What is the world, O soldiers?
　　It is I:
I, this incessant snow,
　　This northern sky;
Soldiers, this solitude
　　Through which we go
　　　Is I.'

'The Raven' is an exemplar of macabre and uncanny nineteenth century Gothic writing, and it is Edgar Allan Poe's most well-known work. Set on a dark December night, it is a tale of psychological horror: a man, pining for the woman he loves, is visited by a mysterious talking raven. The poem charts his descent into darkness and madness, while the raven repeats a single ominous word: 'nevermore'.

Once upon a midnight dreary, while I pondered, weak
     and weary,
Over many a quaint and curious volume of forgotten
     lore –
While I nodded, nearly napping, suddenly there came a
     tapping,
As of some one gently rapping, rapping at my chamber
     door.
''Tis some visitor,' I muttered, 'tapping at my chamber
     door –
          Only this and nothing more.'

Ah, distinctly I remember it was in the bleak December;
And each separate dying ember wrought its ghost upon
     the floor.
Eagerly I wished the morrow; – vainly I had sought to
     borrow
From my books surcease of sorrow – sorrow for the lost
     Lenore –
For the rare and radiant maiden whom the angels name
     Lenore –
          Nameless *here* for evermore.

11

And the silken, sad, uncertain rustling of each purple
   curtain
Thrilled me – filled me with fantastic terrors never felt
   before;
So that now, to still the beating of my heart, I stood
   repeating
"Tis some visitor entreating entrance at my chamber
   door—
Some late visitor entreating entrance at my chamber
   door; –
         This it is and nothing more.'

Presently my soul grew stronger; hesitating then no
   longer,
'Sir,' said I, 'or Madam, truly your forgiveness I implore;
But the fact is I was napping, and so gently you came
   rapping,
And so faintly you came tapping, tapping at my
   chamber door,
That I scarce was sure I heard you' – here I opened wide
   the door; –
         Darkness there and nothing more.

Deep into that darkness peering, long I stood there
   wondering, fearing,
Doubting, dreaming dreams no mortal ever dared to
   dream before;
But the silence was unbroken, and the stillness gave no
   token,
And the only word there spoken was the whispered
   word, 'Lenore?'
This I whispered, and an echo murmured back the
   word, 'Lenore!' –
         Merely this and nothing more.

Back into the chamber turning, all my soul within me burning,
Soon again I heard a tapping somewhat louder than before.
'Surely,' said I, 'surely that is something at my window lattice;
Let me see, then, what thereat is, and this mystery explore –
Let my heart be still a moment and this mystery explore; –
'Tis the wind and nothing more!'

Open here I flung the shutter, when, with many a flirt and flutter,
In there stepped a stately Raven of the saintly days of yore;
Not the least obeisance made he; not a minute stopped or stayed he;
But, with mien of lord or lady, perched above my chamber door –
Perched upon a bust of Pallas just above my chamber door –
Perched, and sat, and nothing more.

Then this ebony bird beguiling my sad fancy into smiling,
By the grave and stern decorum of the countenance it wore,
'Though thy crest be shorn and shaven, thou,' I said, 'art sure no craven,
Ghastly grim and ancient Raven wandering from the Nightly shore –
Tell me what thy lordly name is on the Night's Plutonian shore!'
Quoth the Raven 'Nevermore.'

13

Much I marvelled this ungainly fowl to hear discourse
    so plainly,
Though its answer little meaning – little relevancy bore;
For we cannot help agreeing that no living human being
Ever yet was blessed with seeing bird above his chamber
    door –
Bird or beast upon the sculptured bust above his
    chamber door,
        With such name as 'Nevermore'.

But the Raven, sitting lonely on the placid bust, spoke
    only
That one word, as if his soul in that one word he did
    outpour.
Nothing farther then he uttered – not a feather then he
    fluttered –
Till I scarcely more than muttered 'Other friends have
    flown before –
On the morrow *he* will leave me, as my Hopes have
    flown before.'
        Then the bird said 'Nevermore.'

Startled at the stillness broken by reply so aptly spoken,
'Doubtless,' said I, 'what it utters is its only stock and
    store
Caught from some unhappy master whom unmerciful
    Disaster
Followed fast and followed faster till his songs one
    burden bore –
Till the dirges of his Hope that melancholy burden bore
        Of "Never – nevermore".'

But the Raven still beguiling my sad fancy into smiling,
Straight I wheeled a cushioned seat in front of bird, and
    bust and door;
Then, upon the velvet sinking, I betook myself to linking
Fancy unto fancy, thinking what this ominous bird of
    yore —
What this grim, ungainly, ghastly, gaunt, and ominous
    bird of yore
        Meant in croaking 'Nevermore.'

This I sat engaged in guessing, but no syllable
    expressing
To the fowl whose fiery eyes now burned into my
    bosom's core;
This and more I sat divining, with my head at ease
    reclining
On the cushion's velvet lining that the lamp-light
    gloated o'er,
But whose velvet-violet lining with the lamp-light
    gloating o'er,
        She shall press, ah, nevermore!

Then, methought, the air grew denser, perfumed from
    an unseen censer
Swung by seraphim whose foot-falls tinkled on the
    tufted floor.
'Wretch,' I cried, 'thy God hath lent thee – by these
    angels he hath sent thee
Respite – respite and nepenthe from thy memories of
    Lenore;
Quaff, oh quaff this kind nepenthe and forget this lost
    Lenore!'
        Quoth the Raven 'Nevermore.'

'Prophet!' said I, 'thing of evil! – prophet still, if bird or
   devil! –
Whether Tempter sent, or whether tempest tossed thee
   here ashore,
Desolate yet all undaunted, on this desert land enchanted –
On this home by Horror haunted – tell me truly, I
   implore –
Is there – is there balm in Gilead? – tell me – tell me, I
   implore!'
         Quoth the Raven 'Nevermore.'

'Prophet!' said I, 'thing of evil! – prophet still, if bird or
   devil!
By that Heaven that bends above us – by that God we
   both adore –
Tell this soul with sorrow laden if, within the distant
   Aidenn,
It shall clasp a sainted maiden whom the angels name
   Lenore –
Clasp a rare and radiant maiden whom the angels name
   Lenore.'
         Quoth the Raven 'Nevermore.'

'Be that word our sign of parting, bird or fiend!' I
   shrieked, upstarting –
'Get thee back into the tempest and the Night's
   Plutonian shore!
Leave no black plume as a token of that lie thy soul hath
   spoken!
Leave my loneliness unbroken! – quit the bust above
   my door!
Take thy beak from out my heart, and take thy form
   from off my door!'
         Quoth the Raven 'Nevermore.'

And the Raven, never flitting, still is sitting, *still* is
    sitting
On the pallid bust of Pallas just above my chamber
    door;
And his eyes have all the seeming of a demon's that is
    dreaming,
And the lamp-light o'er him streaming throws his
    shadow on the floor;
And my soul from out that shadow that lies floating on
    the floor
        Shall be lifted – nevermore!

4 December · The Witch ·
Mary Elizabeth Coleridge

The 'witch' of the poem isn't so much a mystical or
magical being as she is a tired old woman, suffering
from exposure to the cold. By labelling her a witch,
Coleridge seems to be making a comment about
women's role in Victorian society, and their appearance
in the eyes of suspicious outsiders.

I have walked a great while over the snow,
And I am not tall nor strong.
My clothes are wet, and my teeth are set,
And the way was hard and long.
I have wandered over the fruitful earth,
But I never came here before.
Oh, lift me over the threshold, and let me in at the door!

The cutting wind is a cruel foe.
I dare not stand in the blast.
My hands are stone, and my voice a groan,
And the worst of death is past.
I am but a little maiden still,
My little white feet are sore.
Oh, lift me over the threshold, and let me in at the door!

Her voice was the voice that women have,
Who plead for their heart's desire.
She came – she came – and the quivering flame
Sunk and died in the fire.
It never was lit again on my hearth
Since I hurried across the floor,
To lift her over the threshold, and let her in at the door.

George Mpanga, better known by his stage name George
the Poet, is a British spoken-word artist, whose poetry
focuses on political and social issues. This poem talks
about the importance and value of children in society.

A child is not a portion of an adult.
It's not a partial being.
A child is an absolute person,
An entire life.

The fact that the child is developing
Doesn't mean it's incomplete.
This just makes it especially important for the
Child to drink and eat, and get a decent wink of sleep,
Many children are given less than children deserve;
Such is the world they entered at birth.
But all it takes is one friend . . . one friend
Who's willing to go to the end of the earth.

For children in the hardest circumstances,
A friend who gives in to no resistance.
Whether down the road or around the globe.
One who's prepared to go the distance,
One who's not scared to show persistence.
No task is too tall, no ask is too small
To send through . . . to attend to.
You could be a friend, too.
Go to the ends of the Earth, for children.

5 December · Mary Celeste · Judith Nicholls

On 5 December 1872, the American ship *Mary Celeste* was discovered washed up on the shores of the Azores islands. The crew were nowhere to be seen, though their belongings and the ship's cargo remained undisturbed, and the ship itself was still seaworthy. None of the crew were ever seen or heard from again, and the fate of the *Mary Celeste*'s sailors remains a mystery to this very day.

Only the wind sings
in the riggings,
the hull creaks a lullaby;
a sail lifts gently
like a message
pinned to a vacant sky.
The wheel turns
over bare decks,
shirts flap on a line;
only the song of the lapping waves
beats steady time . . .

First mate,
off-duty from
the long dawn watch, begins
a letter to his wife, daydreams
of home.

The Captain's wife is late;
the child did not sleep
and breakfast has passed . . .

She, too, is missing home;
sits down at last to eat,
but can't quite force
the porridge down.
She swallows hard,
slices the top from her egg.

The second mate
is happy
A four-hour sleep,
full stomach
and a quiet sea
are all he craves

The child now sleeps, at last,
head firmly pressed into her pillow
in a deep sea-dream.

Then why are the gulls wheeling
like vultures in the sky?
Why was the child snatched
from her sleep? What drew
the Captain's cry?

Only the wind replies
in the rigging,
and the hull creaks and sighs,
a sail spells out its message
over silent skies.
The wheel still turns
over bare decks,
shirts blow on the line;
the siren-song of lapping waves
still echoes over time.

☾ 5 December · Snow and Snow · Ted Hughes

In this poem Ted Hughes uses personification to
describe the snow. Here, he imagines different types of
snowfall to be different kinds of people, even picturing
their clothing.

Snow is sometimes a she, a soft one.
Her kiss on your cheek, her finger on your sleeve
In early December, on a warm evening,
And you turn to meet her, saying 'It's snowing!'
But it is not. And nobody's there.
Empty and calm is the air.

Sometimes the snow is a he, a sly one.
Weakly he signs the dry stone with a damp spot.
Waifish he floats and touches the pond and is not.
Treacherous-beggarly he falters, and taps at the
    window.
A little longer he clings to the grass-blade tip
Getting his grip.

Then how she leans, how furry foxwrap she nestles
The sky with her warm, and the earth with her
    softness.
How her lit crowding fairylands sink through the
    space-silence
To build her palace, till it twinkles in starlight –
Too frail for a foot
Or a crumb of soot.

Then how his muffled armies move in all night
And we wake and every road is blockaded
Every hill taken and every farm occupied
And the white glare of his tents is on the ceiling.
And all that dull blue day and on into the gloaming
We have to watch more coming.

Then everything in the rubbish-heaped world
Is a bridesmaid at her miracle.
Dunghills and crumbly dark old barns are bowed in
    the chapel of her sparkle.
The gruesome boggy cellars of the wood
Are a wedding of lace
Now taking place.

6 December · On Raglan Road ·
Patrick Kavanagh

On this date in 1921, the Irish Free State was formed as an independent state following the Irish War of Independence. It comprised 26 of the 32 Irish counties. The remainder formed Northern Ireland, and thus began the split between British-ruled Northern Ireland and the Republic of Ireland. Ragland Road is a street in Dublin. The poem, published in 1946, was later set to music by the Dubliners and has since been sung by performers from Billy Bragg to Sinead O'Connor and Ed Sheeran.

On Raglan Road on an autumn day I met her first and knew
That her dark hair would weave a snare that I might one day rue;
I saw the danger, yet I walked along the enchanted way,
And I said, let grief be a fallen leaf at the dawning of the day.

On Grafton Street in November we tripped lightly along the ledge
Of the deep ravine where can be seen the worth of passion's pledge,
The Queen of Hearts still making tarts and I not making hay –
O I loved too much and by such and such is happiness thrown away.

25

I gave her gifts of the mind, I gave her the secret sign
that's known
To the artists who have known the true gods of sound
and stone
And word and tint. I did not stint for I gave her poems
to say.
With her own name there and her own dark hair like
clouds over fields of May.

On a quiet street where old ghosts meet I see her
walking now
Away from me so hurriedly my reason must allow
That I had wooed not as I should a creature made of
clay –
When the angel woos the clay he'd lose his wings at the
dawn
of day.

This poem from 1957 is based upon a dream that Ted
Hughes had when he was a student. Hughes wasn't
enjoying his English degree, and he dreamed that a fox
came to him as a representative of the poets he was
studying, telling him to stop. He then changed degree
courses to Anthropology, the study of human societies
through time.

> I imagine this midnight moment's forest:
> Something else is alive
> Beside the clock's loneliness
> And this blank page where my fingers move.
>
> Through the window I see no star:
> Something more near
> though deeper within darkness
> Is entering the loneliness:
>
> Cold, delicately as the dark snow
> A fox's nose touches twig, leaf;
> Two eyes serve a movement, that now
> And again now, and now, and now
>
> Sets neat prints into the snow
> Between trees, and warily a lame
> Shadow lags by stump and in hollow
> Of a body that is bold to come

27

Across clearings, an eye,
A widening deepening greenness,
Brilliantly, concentratedly,
Coming about its own business

Till, with a sudden sharp hot stink of fox,
It enters the dark hole of the head.
The window is starless still; the clock ticks,
The page is printed.

7 December · The Darkling Thrush · Thomas Hardy

One of Hardy's most acclaimed poems, 'The Darkling Thrush' was originally titled 'The Century's End, 1900'. Like many of Hardy's poems, this one is filled with rich natural imagery.

I leant upon a coppice gate
    When Frost was spectre-grey,
And Winter's dregs made desolate
    The weakening eye of day.
The tangled bine-stems scored the sky
    Like strings of broken lyres,
And all mankind that haunted nigh
    Had sought their household fires.

The land's sharp features seemed to be
    The Century's corpse outleant,
His crypt the cloudy canopy,
    The wind his death-lament.
The ancient pulse of germ and birth
    Was shrunken hard and dry,
And every spirit upon earth
    Seemed fervourless as I.

At once a voice arose among
    The bleak twigs overhead
In a full-hearted evensong
    Of joy illimited;
An aged thrush, frail, gaunt, and small,
    In blast-beruffled plume,
Had chosen thus to fling his soul
    Upon the growing gloom.

So little cause for carollings
    Of such ecstatic sound
Was written on terrestrial things
    Afar or nigh around,
That I could think there trembled through
    His happy good-night air
Some blessed Hope, whereof he knew
    And I was unaware.

7 December · The Death of the Ball Turret Gunner · Randall Jarrell

On this day in 1941, Japanese air forces bombed a US military base at Pearl Harbor, Hawaii. It was intended as a pre-emptive strike by the Japanese government, which was allied with the Nazis during the Second World War. As the first attack on American soil, it prompted American entry into the war. This poem, told from the perspective of a dead American aircraft gunner, is unflinching in its observations of the cruel realities of war.

From my mother's sleep I fell into the State,
And I hunched in its belly till my wet fur froze.
Six miles from earth, loosed from its dream of life,
I woke to black flak and the nightmare fighters.
When I died they washed me out of the turret with a hose.

8 December · Embarkation, 1942 ·
John Jarmain

This poem captures a quieter period during a soldier's experience of war. It tells of the night-time departure of the soldiers from familiar terrain to foreign shores. Tension mounts silently and slowly as they near the scene of combat, leaving 'the things we know', and not knowing what may await them.

In undetected trains we left our land
At evening secretly, from wayside stations.
None knew our place of parting; no pale hand
Waved as we went, not one friend said farewell.
But grouped on weed-grown platforms
Only a few officials holding watches
Noted the stealthy hour of our departing,
And, as we went, turned back to their hotel.

With blinds drawn down we left the things we know,
The simple fields, the homely ricks and yards;
Passed willows greyly bunching to the moon
And English towns. But in our blindfold train
Already those were far and long ago,
Stored quiet pictures which the mind must keep:
We saw them not. Instead we played at cards,
Or strangely dropped asleep.

Then in a callow dawn we stood in lines
Like foreigners on bare and unknown quays,
Till someone bravely into the hollow of waiting
Cast a timid wisp of song;
It moved along the lines of patient soldiers
Like a secret passed from mouth to mouth
And slowly gave us ease;
In our whispered singing courage was set free,
We were banded once more and strong.
So we sang as our ship set sail,
Sang our own songs, and leaning on the rail
Waved to the workmen on the slipping quay
And then again to us for fellowship.

☾ 8 December · Birds at Winter Nightfall · Thomas Hardy

Here, Thomas Hardy uses repetition to create a feeling of excitement and joy. Although the birds themselves are never described, we know that they have been there because the berries – one of their favourite snacks – have all disappeared.

Around the house the flakes fly faster,
And all the berries now are gone
From holly and cotoneaster
Around the house. The flakes fly! – faster
Shutting indoors that crumb-outcaster
We used to see upon the lawn
Around the house. The flakes fly faster,
And all the berries now are gone!

9 December · Some Questions You Might Ask · Mary Oliver

The very best poems are those that invite us to
consider our world anew; they remind us of its many
wonders and challenge us to question and reflect on
familiar things. Mary Oliver's poem on the nature of
the soul performs a tightrope walk between silliness
and seriousness – many of the questions might seem
comical on the surface, but think about them for a
few moments and you may find they reveal a certain
profundity . . .

Is the soul solid, like iron?
Or is it tender and breakable, like
the wings of a moth in the beak of the owl?
Who has it, and who doesn't?
I keep looking around me.
The face of the moose is as sad
as the face of Jesus.
The swan opens her white wings slowly.
In the fall, the black bear carries leaves into the
    darkness.
One question leads to another.
Does it have a shape?
Like an iceberg?
Like the eye of a hummingbird?
Does it have one lung, like the snake and the scallop?
Why should I have it, and not the anteater
who loves her children?
Why should I have it, and not the camel?
Come to think of it, what about the maple trees?

What about the blue iris?
What about all the little stones, sitting alone in the
    moonlight?
What about roses, and lemons, and their shining
    leaves?
What about the grass?

Laurie Lee was an English writer who grew up in the Slad Valley in Gloucestershire, and his poems are admired for capturing both the wartime uncertainty of the 1940s and the beauty and peace of the English countryside. In this poem, Lee describes an experience he had with an owl, something he described later as a 'miracle visitation'.

On eves of cold, when slow coal fires,
rooted in basements, burn and branch,
brushing with smoke the city air;
When quartered moons pale in the sky,
and neons glow along the dark
like deadly nightshade on a briar;
Above the muffled traffic then
I hear the owl, and at his note
I shudder in my private chair.
For like an auger he has come
to roost among our crumbling walls,
his blooded talons sheathed in fur.
Some secret lure of time it seems
has called him from his country wastes
to hunt a newer wasteland here.
And where the candelabra swung
bright with the dancers' thousand eyes,
now his black, hooded pupils stare,
And where the silk-shoed lovers ran
with dust of diamonds in their hair,
he opens now his silent wing,
And, like a stroke of doom, drops down,
and swoops across the empty hall,
and plucks a quick mouse off the stair . . .

⚜ 10 December · Refugee Blues · W. H. Auden

Human Rights Day falls on 10 December every year. It is a United Nations campaign to defend the rights of those who are oppressed, disrespected or discriminated against. Auden's wartime poem conveys a sense of what it is like to have your most basic human rights denied, and to be an outsider wherever you go.

Say this city has ten million souls,
Some are living in mansions, some are living in holes:
Yet there's no place for us, my dear, yet there's no
place for us.

Once we had a country and we thought it fair,
Look in the atlas and you'll find it there:
We cannot go there now, my dear, we cannot go there
now.

In the village churchyard there grows an old yew,
Every spring it blossoms anew:
Old passports can't do that, my dear, old passports
can't do that.

The consul banged the table and said,
'If you've got no passport you're officially dead':
But we are still alive, my dear, but we are still alive.

Went to a committee; they offered me a chair;
Asked me politely to return next year:
But where shall we go to-day, my dear, but where shall
we go to-day?

Came to a public meeting; the speaker got up and said;
'If we let them in, they will steal our daily bread':
He was talking of you and me, my dear, he was talking
  of you and me.

Thought I heard the thunder rumbling in the sky;
It was Hitler over Europe, saying, 'They must die':
O we were in his mind, my dear, O we were in his
  mind.

Saw a poodle in a jacket fastened with a pin,
Saw a door opened and a cat let in:
But they weren't German Jews, my dear, but they
  weren't German Jews.

Went down the harbour and stood upon the quay,
Saw the fish swimming as if they were free:
Only ten feet away, my dear, only ten feet away.

Walked through a wood, saw the birds in the trees;
They had no politicians and sang at their ease:
They weren't the human race, my dear, they weren't
  the human race.

Dreamed I saw a building with a thousand floors,
A thousand windows and a thousand doors:
Not one of them was ours, my dear, not one of them
  was ours.

Stood on a great plain in the falling snow;
Ten thousand soldiers marched to and fro:
Looking for you and me, my dear, looking for you and
  me.

☪ 10 December · Light the Festive Candles · Aileen Lucia Fisher

In this poem, Aileen Lucia Fisher uses each of the stanzas to symbolize the lighting of the nine candles that make up the menorah, a special-nine branch candle holder that is an important part of the Hanukkah celebrations. Hanukkah is a Jewish festival that starts on the 25th day of the Hebrew month of Kislah (usually between late November and late December in the Gregorian calendar) and it lasts for eight days. The festival celebrates the victory of the Maccabees – the Jewish patriots – over the Seleucid army, which was far larger. It also celebrates a miracle that occurred, where a single day's supply of olive oil allowed the menorah in the Temple in Jerusalem to remain alight for eight days.

(For Hanukkah)

Light the first of eight tonight –
the farthest candle to the right.

Light the first and second, too,
when tomorrow's day is through.

Then light three, and then light four –
every dusk one candle more

Till all eight burn bright and high,
honoring a day gone by

40

When the Temple was restored,
rescued from the Syrian lord,
And an eight-day feast proclaimed –
The Festival of Lights – well named

To celebrate the joyous day
when we regained the right to pray
to our one God in our own way.

☀ 11 December · Don't Quit · John Greenleaf Whittier

On this day in 1936, Edward VIII abdicated. He had been king for just under a year when he gave up the throne in order to marry Wallis Simpson, a twice-divorced American woman. His abdication was the first entirely voluntary resignation of the throne of England in history.

When things go wrong as they sometimes will,
When the road you're trudging seems all uphill,
When the funds are low and the debts are high
And you want to smile, but you have to sigh,
When care is pressing you down a bit,
Rest, if you must, but don't you quit.

Life is queer with its twists and turns,
As everyone of us sometimes learns,
And many a failure turns about
When he might have won had he stuck it out,
Don't give up though the pace seems slow –
You may succeed with another blow.

Success is failure turned inside out –
The silver tint of the clouds of doubt,
And you never can tell how close you are,
It may be near when it seems so far,
So stick to the fight when you're hardest hit –
It's when things seem worst that you must not quit.

For all the sad words of tongue or pen,
The saddest are these: 'It might have been!'

☾ 11 December · Remembering Snow ·
Brian Patten

Isn't it strange how a snowfall seems to change everything? In this poem, Brian Patten's narrator describes a snowy night that transforms the 'grubby little street' that he knows so well into somewhere unrecognizable, almost otherworldly, in its shimmering beauty.

I did not sleep last night.
The falling snow was beautiful and white.
I dressed, sneaked down the stairs
And opened wide the door.
I had not seen such snow before.
Our grubby little street had gone;
The world was brand-new, and everywhere
There was a pureness in the air.
I felt such peace. Watching every flake
I felt more and more awake.
I thought I'd learned all there was to know
About the trillion million different kinds
Of swirling frosty falling flakes of snow.
But that was not so.
I had not known how vividly it lit
The world with such a peaceful glow.
Upstairs my mother slept.
I could not drag myself away from that sight
To call her down and have her share
That mute miracle of snow.
It seemed to fall for me alone.
How beautiful our grubby little street had grown!

12 December · Snow in the Suburbs · Thomas Hardy

In this poem, Thomas Hardy is describing a snowy
scene in the suburbs. Although the poem's human
speaker is enjoying the snow, it isn't quite as much
fun for the animals stuck outside in it, as shown by the
comical image of the sparrow stuck under a snowfall the
same size as itself and the black cat seeking shelter.

Every branch big with it,
Bent every twig with it;
Every fork like a white web-foot;
Every street and pavement mute:
Some flakes have lost their way, and grope back upward
    when
Meeting those meandering down they turn and descend
    again.
The palings are glued together like a wall,
And there is no waft of wind with the fleecy fall.

A sparrow enters the tree,
Whereon immediately
A snow-lump thrice his own slight size
Descends on him and showers his head and eye
And overturns him,
And near inurns him,
And lights on a nether twig, when its brush
Starts off a volley of other lodging lumps with a rush.

The steps are a blanched slope,
Up which, with feeble hope,
A black cat comes, wide-eyed and thin;
And we take him in.

When we think of sleigh bells, we might be thinking of cosy Christmassy images of pleasure-filled rides in the snow. But Poe, a great master of gothic poetry – that is, poetry that focuses on darkness and horror – does something quite different. Through the obsessive repetition of words, including the bells themselves, Poe's story of an icy winter night is a tale of madness and melancholy.

1

Hear the sledges with the bells –
Silver bells!
What a world of merriment their melody foretells!
How they tinkle, tinkle, tinkle,
In the icy air of night!
While the stars that oversprinkle
All the Heavens, seem to twinkle
With a crystalline delight;
Keeping time, time, time,
In a sort of Runic rhyme,
To the tintinabulation that so musically wells
From the bells, bells, bells, bells,
Bells, bells, bells –
From the jingling and the tinkling of the bells.

Hear the mellow wedding bells –
Golden bells!
What a world of happiness their harmony foretells!
Through the balmy air of night
How they ring out their delight! –
From the molten-golden notes,
And all in tune,
What a liquid ditty floats
To the turtle-dove that listens, while she gloats
On the moon!
Oh, from out the sounding cells,
What a gush of euphony voluminously wells!
How it swells!
How it dwells
On the Future! – how it tells
Of the rapture that impels
To the swinging and the ringing
Of the bells, bells, bells! –
Of the bells, bells, bells, bells,
Bells, bells, bells –
To the rhyming and the chiming of the bells!

3

Hear the loud alarum bells –
Brazen bells!
What tale of terror, now, their turbulency tells!
In the startled ear of Night
How they scream out their affright!
Too much horrified to speak,
They can only shriek, shriek,
Out of tune,
In a clamorous appealing to the mercy of the fire –
In a mad expostulation with the deaf and frantic fire,
Leaping higher, higher, higher,
With a desperate desire,
And a resolute endeavor
Now – now to sit, or never,
By the side of the pale-faced moon.
Oh, the bells, bells, bells!
What a tale their terror tells
Of despair!
How they clang and clash and roar!
What a horror they outpour
In the bosom of the palpitating air!
Yet the ear, it fully knows,
By the twanging,
And the clanging,
How the danger ebbs and flows: –
Yes, the ear distinctly tells,
In the jangling,
And the wrangling,
How the danger sinks and swells,
By the sinking or the swelling in the anger of the bells –
Of the bells –
Of the bells, bells, bells, bells,

Bells, bells, bells —
In the clamor and the clangour of the bells!

4

Hear the tolling of the bells —
    Iron bells!
What a world of solemn thought their monody
compels!
    In the silence of the night
    How we shiver with affright
At the melancholy meaning of their tone!
    For every sound that floats
    From the rust within their throats
        Is a groan.
    And the people — ah, the people
    They that dwell up in the steeple,
        All alone,
    And who, tolling, tolling, tolling,
        In that muffled monotone,
    Feel a glory in so rolling
        On the human heart a stone —
They are neither man nor woman —
They are neither brute nor human,
        They are Ghouls: —
And their king it is who tolls: —
And he rolls, rolls, rolls, rolls,
    A Pæan from the bells!
    And his merry bosom swells
        With the Pæan of the bells!
    And he dances, and he yells;
Keeping time, time, time,
In a sort of Runic rhyme,
    To the Pæan of the bells —

Of the bells: –
Keeping time, time, time,
In a sort of Runic rhyme,
   To the throbbing of the bells –
Of the bells, bells, bells –
   To the sobbing of the bells: –
Keeping time, time, time,
   As he knells, knells, knells,
In a happy Runic rhyme,
   To the rolling of the bells –
Of the bells, bells, bells: –
   To the tolling of the bells,
Of the bells, bells, bells, bells,
   Bells, bells, bells –
To the moaning and the groaning of the bells.

13 December · *from* The Prelude · William Wordsworth

In this passage, an extract from his autobiographical work *The Prelude*, Wordsworth remembers a happy evening skating at sunset in Winter during his childhood in the Lake District. He recalls the joy of skating with his companions, capturing the energy and excitement as he compares the skaters to chasing hounds, but he is set apart from the group as he skates off alone. While skating solo, he is able to appreciate the sublime, awe-inspiring wonder of the mountains and the lakes that surround him, a familiar theme in his poetry.

And in the frosty season, when the sun
Was set, and visible for many a mile
The cottage windows blazed through twilight gloom,
I heeded not their summons: happy time
It was indeed for all of us – for me
It was a time of rapture! Clear and loud
The village clock tolled six, – I wheeled about,
Proud and exulting like an untired horse
That cares not for his home. All shod with steel,
We hissed along the polished ice in games
Confederate, imitative of the chase
And woodland pleasures, – the resounding horn,
The pack loud chiming, and the hunted hare.
So through the darkness and the cold we flew,
And not a voice was idle; with the din
Smitten, the precipices rang aloud;

The leafless trees and every icy crag
Tinkled like iron; while far distant hills
Into the tumult sent an alien sound
Of melancholy not unnoticed, while the stars
Eastward were sparkling clear, and in the west
The orange sky of evening died away.
Not seldom from the uproar I retired
Into a silent bay, or sportively
Glanced sideway, leaving the tumultuous throng,
To cut across the reflex of a star
That fled, and, flying still before me, gleamed
Upon the glassy plain; and oftentimes,
When we had given our bodies to the wind,
And all the shadowy banks on either side
Came sweeping through the darkness, spinning still
The rapid line of motion, then at once
Have I, reclining back upon my heels,
Stopped short; yet still the solitary cliffs
Wheeled by me – even as if the earth had rolled
With visible motion her diurnal round!
Behind me did they stretch in solemn train,
Feebler and feebler, and I stood and watched
Till all was tranquil as a dreamless sleep.

13 December · The Oxen · Thomas Hardy

It is finally time to start thinking about Christmas. This poem by Hardy is a subtle discussion of the nature of faith; it might be far-fetched to imagine oxen kneeling to the new-born baby Jesus, but he still wants to believe it might be true.

Christmas Eve, and twelve of the clock.
　'Now they are all on their knees,'
An elder said as we sat in a flock
　By the embers in hearthside ease.

We pictured the meek mild creatures where
　They dwelt in their strawy pen,
Nor did it occur to one of us there
　To doubt they were kneeling then.

So fair a fancy few would weave
　In these years! Yet, I feel,
If someone said on Christmas Eve,
　'Come; see the oxen kneel

'In the lonely barton by yonder coomb
　Our childhood used to know,'
I should go with him in the gloom,
　Hoping it might be so.

✹ 14 December · Antarctica · Derek Mahon

On 14 December 1911, an expedition led by the
Norwegian Roald Amundsen became the first party
to reach the South Pole, beating a five-man team of
British explorers, led by Captain Scott, who arrived
just weeks later in January 1912. This poem focusses
on Captain Lawrence Oates, a member of that ill-fated
cadre, during what proved to be a fatal return journey.
Knowing he was dying, he decided to walk into a lethal
blizzard rather than slow down his companions. The
first words of this poem are his immortal last words.

'I am just going outside and may be some time.'
The others nod, pretending not to know.
At the heart of the ridiculous, the sublime.

He leaves them reading and begins to climb,
Goading his ghost into the howling snow;
He is just going outside and may be some time.

The tent recedes beneath its crust of rime
And frostbite is replaced by vertigo:
At the heart of the ridiculous, the sublime.

Need we consider it some sort of crime,
This numb self-sacrifice of the weakest? No,
He is just going outside and may be some time –

In fact, for ever. Solitary enzyme,
Though the night yield no glimmer there will glow,
At the heart of the ridiculous, the sublime.

He takes leave of the earthly pantomime
Quietly, knowing it is time to go.
'I am just going outside and may be some time.'
At the heart of the ridiculous, the sublime.

Christina Rossetti

Christina Rossetti was a poet who, as well as writing
longer works, also published a book of nursery rhymes,
Sing-Song. Although this poem has a jaunty feel,
due to its short length and its 'sing-song' structure, it
creates a thoughtful atmosphere. Rossetti was a devoted
Christian, and the call-and-response style of the poem
is similar to the way some prayers are phrased in
Christian church services, called 'catechisms'.

What are heavy? Sea-sand and sorrow:
What are brief? To-day and to-morrow:
What are frail? Spring blossoms and youth:
What are deep? The ocean and truth.

15 December • Forecasts • Jean Kenward

The narrator of this poem is looking for signs and symbols of things to come – forecasting. What begins as a hunt for signs of snow ends as something quite different: a search for signs of hope.

There are berries this year on the holly.
It wasn't always so.
They may be simply a forecast –
forecast of snow.

There's frost on the sill. I've seen it
glitter with diamond light.
It's slippery, too, the traveller
must watch his step tonight.

There's a moon as big as a melon,
and far-off – O, how far –
flickering on the horizon . . .
a fresh, and different, star . . .

In the heart of man is a coldness.
Through a crack in the stable door
there glimmers a new dominion.

Even ice can thaw.

☾ 15 December · Slip into Sleep · Mandy Coe

Do you ever roll around in bed, unable to get to sleep
in spite of every effort at lying still and counting sheep?
This meditative poem by Mandy Coe, with its soothing
use of repetition and single rhyme of 'sleep' and 'deep',
is a brilliant one to remember when you climb into bed.

Slip your toes into sleep
Slip your heels into sleep
Slip your knees into sleep
Slip your hips into sleep
Breathe soft, breathe deep
Slip into sleep

Slip your middle into sleep
Slip your chest into sleep
Slip your shoulders into sleep
Slip your arms into sleep
Breathe soft, breathe deep
Slip into sleep

Slip your elbows into sleep
Slip your wrists into sleep
Slip your fingers into sleep
Breathe soft, breathe deep
Slip into sleep

Slip your neck into sleep
Slip your chin into sleep
Slip your lips into sleep
Breathe soft, breathe deep
Slip into sleep

Slip your nose into sleep
Slip your eyes into sleep
Slip your hair into sleep
Breathe soft, breathe deep
Slip into sleep

16 December · little tree · E. E. Cummings

In this poem, Cummings takes on the voice of a child to hold an imaginary conversation with a Christmas tree. The shape of the words on the page seems to branch out like a fir tree, and the two strange gaps between words take on the appearance of shiny baubles.

little tree
little silent Christmas tree
you are so little
you are more like a flower

who found you in the green forest
and were you very sorry to come away?
see   i will comfort you
because you smell so sweetly

i will kiss your cool bark
and hug you safe and tight
just as your mother would,
only don't be afraid

look   the spangles
that sleep all the year in a dark box
dreaming of being taken out and allowed to shine,
the balls the chains red and gold the fluffy threads,

put up your little arms
and i'll give them all to you to hold
every finger shall have its ring
and there won't be a single place dark or unhappy

then when you're quite dressed
you'll stand in the window for everyone to see
and how they'll stare!
oh but you'll be very proud

and my little sister and i will take hands
and looking up at our beautiful tree
we'll dance and sing
'Noel Noel'

🌙 16 December · In the Last Quarter · Dave Calder

Haunted by a huge bright moon and featuring a strange magical event, this poem by Dave Calder is another that is perfect for night-time.

She sat at the table under the small light.
Outside the window the moon rose huge and yellow,
   slow, swollen, weighing down the night.

She turned the pages of a book, pages that
were dry and stiff; and the book's spine creaked each
   time she moved her hand to hold them flat.

From somewhere a wind began to stir the room – cups
   chinked softly on their hooks, in a vase the dusty
   flowers brushed together; soon

the shelves, the pots and plates, began to tremble
with the edgy aching sound of something about to break
   and under the swaying lamp she could no longer tell

one word from another. She put her head down,
one ear pressed on the book as if to listen, and watched
   leaves twist across the floor, drift into mounds

around her feet and up against the wall;
leaves swirling and falling till the room was lost in them
   and their rustling whisper like the scurrying of small

62

animals or the parched voices of the dead. And then her
   eyelids fluttered, shut; and the wind also dropped,
   sudden, and in the room everything fell silent.

The lamp hung above her, its shadow didn't change.
   Her chair stopped creaking, and the leaves
lay deep enough to drown in; like tiny hands or flames

the leaves lay from wall to wall, high
as her waist, as the window. Not a sigh. Beyond the
   glass the moon swept, bright and staring, into a
   frozen sky.

17 December · High Flight ·
John Gillespie Magee, Jr.

On this day in 1903, the first ever aeroplane ride took
place near Kitty Hawk, North Carolina. This was thanks
to two mechanically minded brothers called Orville and
Wilbur Wright. 'High Flight' is a sonnet celebrating
the joys of being airborne, written in 1941 by another
American, John Gillespie Magee, Jr. A pilot in the Royal
Canadian Air Force, Magee was only nineteen when he
wrote 'High Flight' on the back of an envelope and sent
it to his parents.

Oh! I have slipped the surly bonds of Earth
And danced the skies on laughter-silvered wings;
Sunward I've climbed, and joined the tumbling mirth
Of sun-split clouds, and done a hundred things
You have not dreamed of: wheeled and soared and swung
High in the sunlit silence. Hov'ring there,
I've chased the shouting wind along, and flung
My eager craft through footless halls of air . . .
Up, up the long, delirious, burning blue
I've topped the wind-swept heights with easy grace
Where never lark nor even eagle flew
And, while with silent lifting mind I've trod
The high untrespassed sanctity of space,
Put out my hand, and touched the face of God.

17 December · Christmas is Coming · Anon.

This traditional nursery rhyme dates back to the nineteenth century at least, and centres around the image of a goose – a popular Christmas dinner for the Victorians. However, it is also a song about charity and sharing, the real spirit of Christmas.

Christmas is coming,
  The geese are getting fat,
Please to put a penny
  In the old man's hat.
If you haven't got a penny,
  A ha'penny will do;
If you haven't got a ha'penny,
  Then God bless you!

18 December · The Computer's First Christmas Card · Edwin Morgan

Computers have become more and more a part of our lives, and we are rarely away from screens these days. Computers can do all sorts of things for us, but, as Edwin Morgan makes clear, it's a very bad idea to trust them with writing your Christmas cards!

jollymerry
hollyberry
jollyberry
merryholly
happyjolly
jollyjelly
jellybelly
bellymerry
hollyheppy
jollyMolly
marryJerry
merryHarry
happyBarry
heppyJarry
bobbyheppy
berryjorry
jorryjolly
moppyjelly
Mollymerry
Jerryjolly
bellyboppy
jorryhoppy

hollymoppy
Barrymerry
Jarryhappy
happyboppy
boppyjolly
jollymerry
merrymerry
merrymerry
merryChris
ammerryasa
Chrismerry
asMERRYCHR
YSANTHEMUM

☾ 18 December • A Week to Christmas • John Cotton

In this poem by John Cotton, the seven rhyming stanzas each represents a day of the week leading up to Christmas.

Sunday with six whole days to go,
How we'll endure it I don't know!

Monday the goodies are in the making,
Spice smells of pudding and mince pies a-baking.

Tuesday, Dad's home late and quiet as a mouse
He smuggles packages into the house.

Wednesday's the day for decorating the tree.
Will the lights work again? We'll have to see!

Thursday's for last minute shopping and hurry,
We've never seen Mum in quite such a flurry!

Friday is Christmas Eve when we'll lie awake
Trying to sleep before the day break.

And that special quiet of Christmas morn
When out there somewhere Christ was born.

19 December • O Little Town of Bethlehem • Phillips Brooks

Phillips Brooks was an American priest, who wrote this popular carol in 1868 after having visited the holy town of Bethlehem three years earlier. The tune to which the carol is now sung was written by Ralph Vaughan Williams in 1903.

O little town of Bethlehem,
    how still we see thee lie;
above thy deep and dreamless sleep
    the silent stars go by.
Yet in thy dark streets shineth
    the everlasting light;
the hopes and fears of all the years
    are met in thee tonight.

For Christ is born of Mary,
    and gathered all above,
while mortals sleep, the angels keep
    their watch of wondering love.
O morning stars together,
    proclaim the holy birth,
and praises sing to God the king,
    and peace to all on earth!

69

How silently, how silently,
    the wondrous gift is given;
so God imparts to human hearts
    the blessings of his heaven.
No ear may hear his coming,
    but in this world of sin,
where meek souls will receive him, still
    the dear Christ enters in.

O holy Child of Bethlehem,
    descend to us, we pray;
cast out our sin, and enter in,
    be born in us today.
We hear the Christmas angels
    the great glad tidings tell;
O come to us, abide with us,
    our Lord Emmanuel!

19 December • Christmas • John Betjeman

John Betjeman was a practising Anglican, and the religious side of his character comes through in some of his poems, particularly those that are inspired by Christmas. This poem both celebrates the secular traditions of the Christmas season, such as the wrapped gifts and decorations, as a time that brings people together, and expresses doubts about the true meaning of the Christian festival, illustrated by the repetition of the rhetorical question 'Is it true?'. The poem is ultimately a hopeful one, however, as Betjeman reveals his faith in the Nativity story, and optimism about the way Christmas can bring people together.

The bells of waiting Advent ring,
   The Tortoise stove is lit again
And lamp-oil light across the night
   Has caught the streaks of winter rain
In many a stained-glass window sheen
From Crimson Lake to Hooker's Green.

The holly in the windy hedge
   And round the Manor House the yew
Will soon be stripped to deck the ledge,
   The altar, font and arch and pew,
So that the villagers can say
'The church looks nice' on Christmas Day.

71

Provincial public houses blaze,
   And Corporation tramcars clang,
On lighted tenements I gaze
   Where paper decorations hang,
And bunting in the red Town Hall
Says 'Merry Christmas to you all'.

And London shops on Christmas Eve
   Are strung with silver bells and flowers
As hurrying clerks the City leave
   To pigeon-haunted classic towers,
And marbled clouds go scudding by
The many-steepled London sky.

And girls in slacks remember Dad,
   And oafish louts remember Mum,
And sleepless children's hearts are glad.
   And Christmas-morning bells say 'Come!'
Even to shining ones who dwell
Safe in the Dorchester Hotel.

And is it true? And is it true?
   This most tremendous tale of all,
Seen in a stained-glass window's hue,
   A Baby in an ox's stall ?
The Maker of the stars and sea
Become a Child on earth for me?

And is it true ? For if it is,
  No loving fingers tying strings
Around those tissued fripperies,
  The sweet and silly Christmas things,
Bath salts and inexpensive scent
And hideous tie so kindly meant,

No love that in a family dwells,
  No carolling in frosty air,
Nor all the steeple-shaking bells
  Can with this single Truth compare –
That God was Man in Palestine
And lives to-day in Bread and Wine.

❄ 20 December · Winter-Time ·
Robert Louis Stevenson

Winter is a season of short days and bitter weather.
Yet in this poem Robert Louis Stevenson also conjures
a sense of wonder – for there are jolly fires and trees
sparkling beautifully with frost, too!

Late lies the wintry sun a-bed,
A frosty, fiery sleepy-head;
Blinks but an hour or two; and then,
A blood-red orange, sets again.

Before the stars have left the skies,
At morning in the dark I rise;
And shivering in my nakedness,
By the cold candle, bathe and dress.

Close by the jolly fire I sit
To warm my frozen bones a bit;
Or with a reindeer-sled, explore
The colder countries round the door.

When to go out, my nurse doth wrap
Me in my comforter and cap;
The cold wind burns my face, and blows
Its frosty pepper up my nose.

Black are my steps on silver sod;
Thick blows my frosty breath abroad;
And tree and house, and hill and lake,
Are frosted like a wedding cake.

20 December · Talking Turkeys ·
Benjamin Zephaniah

Benjamin Zephaniah is a British Jamaican poet, lyricist and writer who often incorporates Jamaican dialect into his work. This poem, and the book of the same name, enjoyed huge success upon their release in 1994.

Be nice to yu turkeys dis christmas
Cos' turkeys just wanna hav fun
Turkeys are cool, turkeys are wicked
An every turkey has a Mum.
Be nice to yu turkeys dis christmas,
Don't eat it, keep it alive,
It could be yu mate, an not on yu plate
Say, Yo! Turkey I'm on your side.

I got lots of friends who are turkeys
An all of dem fear christmas time,
Dey wanna enjoy it, dey say humans destroyed it
An humans are out of dere mind,
Yeah, I got lots of friends who are turkeys
Dey all hav a right to a life,
Not to be caged up an genetically made up
By any farmer an his wife.

Turkeys just wanna play reggae
Turkeys just wanna hip-hop
Can yu imagine a nice young turkey saying,
'I cannot wait for de chop',
Turkeys like getting presents, dey wanna watch
   christmas TV,
Turkeys hav brains an turkeys feel pain
In many ways like yu an me.
I once knew a turkey called
Turkey
He said 'Benji explain to me please,
Who put de turkey in christmas
An what happens to christmas trees?',
I said 'I am not too sure turkey
But it's nothing to do wid Christ Mass
Humans get greedy an waste more dan need be
An business men mek loadsa cash'.

Be nice to yu turkey dis christmas
Invite dem indoors fe sum greens
Let dem eat cake an let dem partake
In a plate of organic grown beans,
Be nice to yu turkey dis christmas
An spare dem de cut of de knife,
Join Turkeys United an dey'll be delighted
An yu will mek new friends 'FOR LIFE'.

21 December · Puzzle · Philip Waddell

On 21 December 1913, the world's first crossword puzzle was printed in the US newspaper the *New York World*. It had been invented by a man from Liverpool, Arthur Wynne. Philip Waddell's poem feeds us cryptic clues, leading up to the puzzle itself.

Count three weeks and you'd be there
in the twelfth month of the year
before the Great War.
Readers saw the first appear
in a Sunday paper called
the *New York World*.
It wasn't a furious word, just cross,
and to this day they puzzle us.

77

This Christmas poem imagines a lasting peace between the adherents of all major religions, 'Baptist and Buddhist, Methodist and Muslim'. The poet finds a remarkable power in the softly spoken word 'peace', which can triumph over war and violence. Angelou, who was recognized throughout her life as a political figure and civil rights activist, concludes the poem by addressing the word 'peace' to her brothers and sisters in the human race, before finally speaking the word to her own soul.

Thunder rumbles in the mountain passes
And lightning rattles the eaves of our houses.
Flood waters await us in our avenues.

Snow falls upon snow, falls upon snow to avalanche
Over unprotected villages.
The sky slips low and grey and threatening.

We question ourselves.
What have we done to so affront nature?
We worry God.
Are you there? Are you there really?
Does the covenant you made with us still hold?

Into this climate of fear and apprehension, Christmas
    enters,
Streaming lights of joy, ringing bells of hope
And singing carols of forgiveness high up in the bright
    air.

The world is encouraged to come away from rancor,
Come the way of friendship.

It is the Glad Season.
Thunder ebbs to silence and lightning sleeps quietly in
    the corner.
Flood waters recede into memory.
Snow becomes a yielding cushion to aid us
As we make our way to higher ground.

Hope is born again in the faces of children
It rides on the shoulders of our aged as they walk into
    their sunsets.
Hope spreads around the earth. Brightening all things,
Even hate which crouches breeding in dark corridors.

In our joy, we think we hear a whisper.
At first it is too soft. Then only half heard.
We listen carefully as it gathers strength.
We hear a sweetness.
The word is Peace.
It is loud now. It is louder.
Louder than the explosion of bombs.

We tremble at the sound. We are thrilled by its
    presence.
It is what we have hungered for.
Not just the absence of war. But, true Peace.
A harmony of spirit, a comfort of courtesies.
Security for our beloveds and their beloveds.

79

We clap hands and welcome the Peace of Christmas.
We beckon this good season to wait a while with us.
We, Baptist and Buddhist, Methodist and Muslim, say
    come. Peace.
Come and fill us and our world with your majesty.
We, the Jew and the Jainist, the Catholic and the
    Confucian,
Implore you, to stay a while with us.
So we may learn by your shimmering light
How to look beyond complexion and see community.

It is Christmas time, a halting of hate time.

On this platform of peace, we can create a language
To translate ourselves to ourselves and to each other.

At this Holy Instant, we celebrate the Birth of Jesus
    Christ
Into the great religions of the world.
We jubilate the precious advent of trust.
We shout with glorious tongues at the coming of hope.
All the earth's tribes loosen their voices
To celebrate the promise of Peace.

We, Angels and Mortals, Believers and Non-Believers,
Look heavenward and speak the word aloud.
Peace. We look at our world and speak the word aloud.
Peace. We look at each other, then into ourselves
And we say without shyness or apology or hesitation.

Peace, My Brother.
Peace, My Sister.
Peace, My Soul.

22 December · The Year's Midnight · Gillian Clarke

Winter solstice – the darkest day of the year in the northern hemisphere – always falls between 21 and 23 December. The days will gradually lengthen again from this point onwards. Gillian Clarke's poem is a voice from the depths of darkness, but it is one that knows that daylight will come again.

The flown, the fallen,
the golden ones,
the deciduous dead, all gone
to ground, to dust, to sand,
borne on the shoulders of the wind.

Listen! They are whispering
now while the world talks,
and the ice melts,
and the seas rise.
Look at the trees!

Every leaf-scar is a bud
expecting a future.
The earth speaks in parables.
The burning bush. The rainbow.
Promises. Promises.

81

Christmas Day is traditionally the celebration of the birth of the baby Jesus, which came at the end of a long and difficult journey for Mary and her husband Joseph. In this poem, Eleanor Farjeon imagines Mary being relieved of the 'burden' of her pregnancy, only to be burdened in a different way, with worries about all that her son will have to bear, as the saviour of mankind.

> My Baby, my Burden,
> Tomorrow the morn
> I shall go lighter
> And you will be born.
>
> I shall go lighter,
> But heavier too
> For seeing the burden
> That falls upon you.
>
> The burden of love,
> The burden of pain,
> I'll see you bear both
> Among men once again.
>
> Tomorrow you'll bear it
> Your burden alone,
> Tonight you've no burden
> That is not my own

My Baby, my Burden,
Tomorrow the morn
I shall go lighter
And you will be born.

23 December · Just Doing My Job · Clare Bevan

December is a time for festive shows, from Christmas plays at school to Nativity scenes at Christingle services. This poem sums up the joy and chaos they entail.

I'm one of Herod's Henchmen.
We don't have much to say,
We just charge through the audience
In a Henchman sort of way.

We all wear woolly helmets
To hide our hair and ears,
And wellingtons sprayed silver
To match our tinfoil spears.

Our swords are made of cardboard
So blood will not be spilled
If we trip and stab a parent
When the hall's completely filled.

We don't look VERY scary,
We're mostly small and shy,
And some of us wear glasses,
But we give the thing a try.

We whisper Henchman noises
While Herod hunts for strangers,
And then we all charge out again
Like nervous Power Rangers.

Yet when the play is over
And Miss is out of breath
We'll charge like Henchmen through the hall
And scare our mums to death.

☾ 23 December • Help Wanted •
Timothy Tocher

This poem by Timothy Tocher takes its inspiration from 'A Visit from St Nicholas', which you can find over the page. Tocher's poem is a comic reinterpretation of the familiar image of Father Christmas and his faithful reindeer, imagining a poster advertising for new reindeer to take over from Dasher, Dancer, Rudolf and the rest.

Santa needs new reindeer.
The first bunch has grown old.
Dasher has arthritis;
Comet hates the cold.
Prancer's sick of staring
at Dancer's big behind.
Cupid married Blitzen
and Donder lost his mind.
Dancer's mad at Vixen
for stepping on his toes.
Vixen's being thrown out –
she laughed at Rudolph's nose.
If you are a reindeer
we hope you will apply.
There is just one tricky part:
You must know how to fly.

24 December · Saturday Night at the Bethlehem Arms · Gareth Owen

It does not need saying that today is Christmas Eve.
This poem is about a pub landlord on a quiet Saturday,
not realizing that the first Christmas is taking place in
his stable.

Very quiet really for a Saturday.
Just the old couple come to visit relations
Who took the double room above the yard
And were both of them in bed by half past nine.
Left me with that other one, the stranger.
Sat like he was set till Domesday at the corner of the bar
Sipping small beer dead slow and keeping mum,
Those beady, tax-collector's eyes of his
On my reflection in the glass behind the bar
Watching me, watching me.
And when he did get round to saying something
His talk was like those lines of gossamer
That fishermen send whispering across the water
To lure and hook unwary fish.
Not my type. And anyway I'd been on the go since five.
Deadbeat I was.
Some of us have a bed to go to, I thought to myself.
I was just about to call Time
When the knock came at the door.
At first I was for turning them away;
We only have two rooms see and both of them were
    taken.
But something desperate in the woman's eyes

Made me think again and I told them,
They could rough it in the barn
If they didn't mind the cows and mules for company.
I know, I know. Soft, that's me.
I yawned, locked up, turned out the lights,
Rinsed my hands to lose the smell of beer.
Went up to bed.
A day like any other.
That's how it is.
Nothing much ever happens here.

24 December · A Visit from St Nicholas · Clement Clarke Moore

'A Visit from St Nicholas' is possibly the one poem which has most influence on modern depictions of St Nicholas, or Santa Claus, across the English-speaking world. It is said that Moore wrote the poem for his family on Christmas Eve, 1822, and never intended for it to be published.

'Twas the night before Christmas, when all through the
    house
Not a creature was stirring, not even a mouse;
The stockings were hung by the chimney with care,
In hopes that St Nicholas soon would be there;
The children were nestled all snug in their beds;
While visions of sugar-plums danced in their heads;
And mamma in her 'kerchief, and I in my cap,
Had just settled our brains for a long winter's nap –
When out on the lawn there arose such a clatter,
I sprang from my bed to see what was the matter.
Away to the window I flew like a flash,
Tore open the shutters and threw up the sash.
The moon on the breast of the new-fallen snow,
Gave a lustre of midday to objects below;
When what to my wondering eyes did appear,
But a miniature sleigh and eight tiny reindeer,
With a little old driver so lively and quick,
I knew in a moment it must be St Nick.
More rapid than eagles his coursers they came,
And he whistled, and shouted, and called them by
    name:
'Now, *Dasher*! now, *Dancer*! now, *Prancer* and *Vixen*!

On, *Comet*! on, *Cupid*! on, *Doner* and *Blitzen*!
To the top of the porch! to the top of the wall!
Now dash away! dash away! dash away all!'
As leaves that before the wild hurricane fly,
When they meet with an obstacle, mount to the sky;
So up to the house-top the coursers they flew
With the sleigh full of toys, and St Nicholas too –
And then, in a twinkling, I heard on the roof
The prancing and pawing of each little hoof.
As I drew in my head, and was turning around,
Down the chimney St Nicholas came with a bound.
He was dressed all in fur, from his head to his foot,
And his clothes were all tarnished with ashes and soot;
A bundle of toys he had flung on his back,
And he looked like a pedlar just opening his pack.
His eyes – how they twinkled! his dimples, how merry!
His cheeks were like roses, his nose like a cherry!
His droll little mouth was drawn up like a bow,
And the beard on his chin was as white as the snow;
The stump of a pipe he held tight in his teeth,
And the smoke, it encircled his head like a wreath;
He had a broad face and a little round belly
That shook, when he laughed, like a bowl full of jelly.
He was chubby and plump, a right jolly old elf,
And I laughed when I saw him, in spite of myself;
A wink of his eye and a twist of his head
Soon gave me to know I had nothing to dread;
He spoke not a word, but went straight to his work,
And filled all the stockings; then turned with a jerk,
And laying his finger aside of his nose,
And giving a nod, up the chimney he rose;
He sprang to his sleigh, to his team gave a whistle,
And away they all flew like the down of a thistle.
But I heard him exclaim, ere he drove out of sight:
'Happy Christmas to all, and to all a good night!'

25 December · I Saw a Stable ·
Mary Elizabeth Coleridge

Today is Christmas Day, a day for family, feasting, and festivities. Amid all the presents and parsnips, though, there is always time for a brief poem. Mary Elizabeth Coleridge's lines on the original meaning of Christmas is perfect for sharing.

I saw a stable, low and very bare,
  A little child in a manger.
The oxen knew Him, had Him in their care,
  To men He was a stranger.
The safety of the world was lying there,
  And the world's danger.

☾ **25 December** · The Twelve Days of Christmas · Anon.

This popular carol was originally published without music, as a poem, in the eighteenth century. 'The Twelve Days of Christmas' run from Christmas Day to the eve of Epiphany on 5 January.

> On the first day of Christmas,
> my true love sent to me
> A partridge in a pear tree.
>
> On the second day of Christmas,
> my true love sent to me
> Two turtle doves,
> And a partridge in a pear tree.
>
> On the third day of Christmas,
> my true love sent to me
> Three French hens,
> Two turtle doves,
> And a partridge in a pear tree.
>
> On the fourth day of Christmas,
> my true love sent to me
> Four calling birds,
> Three French hens,
> Two turtle doves,
> And a partridge in a pear tree.

92

On the fifth day of Christmas,
my true love sent to me
Five golden rings,
Four calling birds,
Three French hens,
Two turtle doves,
And a partridge in a pear tree.

On the sixth day of Christmas,
my true love sent to me
Six geese a-laying,
Five golden rings,
Four calling birds,
Three French hens,
Two turtle doves,
And a partridge in a pear tree.

On the seventh day of Christmas,
my true love sent to me
Seven swans a-swimming,
Six geese a-laying,
Five golden rings,
Four calling birds,
Three French hens,
Two turtle doves,
And a partridge in a pear tree.

On the eighth day of Christmas,
my true love sent to me
Eight maids a-milking,
Seven swans a-swimming,
Six geese a-laying,
Five golden rings,
Four calling birds,
Three French hens,
Two turtle doves,
And a partridge in a pear tree.

On the ninth day of Christmas,
my true love sent to me
Nine ladies dancing,
Eight maids a-milking,
Seven swans a-swimming,
Six geese a-laying,
Five golden rings,
Four calling birds,
Three French hens,
Two turtle doves,
And a partridge in a pear tree.

On the tenth day of Christmas,
my true love sent to me
Ten lords a-leaping,
Nine ladies dancing,
Eight maids a-milking,
Seven swans a-swimming,
Six geese a-laying,
Five golden rings,
Four calling birds,
Three French hens,
Two turtle doves,
And a partridge in a pear tree.

On the eleventh day of Christmas,
my true love sent to me
Eleven pipers piping,
Ten lords a-leaping,
Nine ladies dancing,
Eight maids a-milking,
Seven swans a-swimming,
Six geese a-laying,
Five golden rings,
Four calling birds,
Three French hens,
Two turtle doves,
And a partridge in a pear tree.

On the twelfth day of Christmas,
my true love sent to me
Twelve drummers drumming,
Eleven pipers piping,
Ten lords a-leaping,
Nine ladies dancing,
Eight maids a-milking,
Seven swans a-swimming,
Six geese a-laying,
Five golden rings,
Four calling birds,
Three French hens,
Two turtle doves,
And a partridge in a pear tree!

26 December · Dear True Love ·
U. A. Fanthorpe

This poem is written as a reply to 'The Twelve Days of Christmas'. Just who needs six geese a-laying, anyway?

Leaping and dancing
Means to-ing and fro-ing;
Drummers and pipers –
Loud banging and blowing;
Even a pear-tree
Needs room to grow in.

Goose eggs and gold top
When I'm trying to slim?
And seven swans swimming?
Just where could they swim?

Mine is a small house,
Your gifts are grand;
One ring at a time
Is enough for this hand.

Hens, colly birds, doves,
A gastronome's treat.
But, love, I did tell you,
I've given up meat.

Your fairy-tale presents
Are wasted on me.
Just send me your love
And set all the birds free.

☾ 26 December · King John's Christmas · A. A. Milne

This is a light-hearted idea of how one of the more controversial monarchs of medieval England might have spent Christmas.

King John was not a good man –
　He had his little ways.
And sometimes no one spoke to him
　For days and days and days.
And men who came across him,
　When walking in the town,
Gave him a supercilious stare,
Or passed with noses in the air –
And bad King John stood dumbly there,
　Blushing beneath his crown.

King John was not a good man,
　And no good friends had he.
He stayed in every afternoon . . .
　But no one came to tea.
And, round about December,
　The cards upon his shelf
Which wished him lots of Christmas cheer,
And fortune in the coming year,
Were never from his near and dear,
　But only from himself.
King John was not a good man,
　Yet had his hopes and fears.
They'd given him no present now

97

For years and years and years.
But every year at Christmas,
    While minstrels stood about,
Collecting tribute from the young
For all the songs they might have sung,
He stole away upstairs and hung
    A hopeful stocking out.

King John was not a good man,
    He lived his live aloof;
Alone he thought a message out
    While climbing up the roof.
He wrote it down and propped it
    Against the chimney stack:
'TO ALL AND SUNDRY – NEAR AND FAR –
F. Christmas in particular.'
And signed it not 'Johannes R.'
    But very humbly, 'Jack'.

'I want some crackers,
    And I want some candy;
I think a box of chocolates
    Would come in handy;
I don't mind oranges,
    I do like nuts!
And I SHOULD like a pocket-knife
That really cuts.
And, oh! Father Christmas, if you love me at all,
    Bring me a big, red, india-rubber ball!'

King John was not a good man –
    He wrote this message out,
And gat him to this room again,
    Descending by the spout.
And all that night he lay there,
    A prey to hopes and fears.
    'I think that's him a-coming now!'
    (Anxiety bedewed his brow.)
    'He'll bring one present, anyhow –
    The first I've had for years.'

'Forget about the crackers,
    And forget the candy;
I'm sure a box of chocolates
    Would never come in handy;
I don't like oranges,
    I don't want nuts,
And I HAVE got a pocket-knife
    That almost cuts.
But, oh! Father Christmas, if you love me at all,
Bring me a big, red, india-rubber ball!'

King John was not a good man –
    Next morning when the sun
Rose up to tell a waiting world
    That Christmas had begun,
And people seized their stockings,
    And opened them with glee,
And crackers, toys and games appeared,
And lips with sticky sweets were smeared,
King John said grimly: 'As I feared,
    Nothing again for me!'

'I did want crackers,
  And I did want candy;
I know a box of chocolates
  Would come in handy;
I do love oranges,
  I did want nuts!
I haven't got a pocket-knife -
  Not one that cuts.
And, oh! if Father Christmas, had loved me at all,
He would have brought a big, red, india-rubber ball!'

King John stood by the window,
  And frowned to see below
The happy bands of boys and girls
  All playing in the snow.
A while he stood there watching,
  And envying them all . . .
When through the window big and red
There hurtled by his royal head,
And bounced and fell upon the bed,
  An india-rubber ball!

AND, OH, FATHER CHRISTMAS,
  MY BLESSINGS ON YOU FALL
    FOR BRINGING HIM
    A BIG, RED,
    INDIA-RUBBER
    BALL!

27 December · Reindeer Report ·
U. A. Fanthorpe

In the modern world, Christmas can seem like a small island of peace amid the hectic month of December and the run-up to the new year. U. A. Fanthorpe's poem helps us tick another successful Christmas off the list.

Chimneys: colder.
Flightpaths: busier.
Driver: Christmas (F)
Still baffled by postcodes.

Children: more
And stay up later.
Presents: heavier.
Pay: frozen.

Mission in spite
Of all this:
Accomplished.

☾ 27 December · At Nine of the Night · Charles Causley

In this poem, Charles Causley takes a familiar, snowy Christmas scene and turns it on its head, leaving the reader full of questions. Who is the stranger wrapped in a red cloak? Is it the stable-boy, or is it someone altogether more mysterious?

At nine of the night I opened my door
That stands midway between moor and moor,
And all around me, silver-bright,
I saw that the world had turned to white.

Thick was the snow on field and hedge
And vanished was the river-sedge,
Where winter skilfully had wound
A shining scarf without a sound.

And as I stood and gazed my fill
A stable-boy came down the hill.
With every step I saw him take
Flew at his heel a puff of flake.

His brow was whiter than the hoar,
A beard of freshest snow he wore,
And round about him, snowflake starred,
A red horse-blanket from the yard.

In a red cloak I saw him go,
His back was bent, his step was slow,
And as he laboured through the cold
He seemed a hundred winters old.

I stood and watched the snowy head,
The whiskers white, the cloak of red.
'A Merry Christmas!' I heard him cry.
'The same to you, old friend,' said I.

28 December • *from* Paradise Lost • John Milton

On this day in 1831, Charles Darwin set sail on the ship HMS *Beagle*. The voyage, which went clockwise around the world, lasted almost five years. The countless observations he made of great varieties of species of flora and fauna led to the establishment of his Theory of Evolution. Darwin took several books with him, including a copy of the 1667 epic poem *Paradise Lost* by John Milton which he read obsessively. Here are the very last lines of the poem, describing Adam and Eve's expulsion from Eden.

In either hand the hast'ning angel caught
Our ling'ring parents, and to th' eastern gate
Led them direct, and down the cliff as fast
To the subjected plain; then disappeared.
They looking back, all th' eastern side beheld
Of Paradise, so late thir happy seat,
Waved over by that flaming brand, the gate
With dreadful faces thronged and fiery arms:
Some natural tears they dropped, but wiped them soon;
The world was all before them, where to choose
Their place of rest, and Providence thir guide:
They hand in hand with wand'ring steps and slow,
Through Eden took thir solitary way.

28 December · In the Bleak Midwinter · Christina Rossetti

In the early 1870s, Christina Rossetti wrote this poem in response to an advert in the magazine *Scribner's Monthly* that was looking for a Christmas poem. Rossetti describes the birth of the baby Jesus, before stating that it doesn't matter if you can't afford to give anything expensive or impressive: it's enough just to give your heart. The poem has been set to music many times, and remains a popular Christmas carol.

> In the bleak midwinter
>   Frosty wind made moan,
> Earth stood hard as iron,
>   Water like a stone;
> Snow had fallen, snow on snow,
>   Snow on snow,
> In the bleak midwinter
>   Long ago.
>
> Our God, Heaven cannot hold Him,
>   Nor earth sustain;
> Heaven and earth shall flee away
>   When He comes to reign.
> In the bleak midwinter
>   A stable place sufficed
> The Lord God Almighty,
>   Jesus Christ.

Enough for Him, whom cherubim
    Worship night and day,
A breastful of milk,
    And a mangerful of hay;
Enough for Him, whom angels
    Fall down before,
The ox and ass and camel
    Which adore.

Angels and archangels
    May have gathered there,
Cherubim and seraphim
    Thronged the air;
But His mother only,
    In her maiden bliss,
Worshipped the beloved
    With a kiss.

What can I give Him,
    Poor as I am?
If I were a shepherd,
    I would bring a lamb;
If I were a Wise Man,
    I would do my part;
Yet what I can I give Him:
    Give my heart.

29 December · The Year ·
Ella Wheeler Wilcox

In these rhyming couplets, Ella Wheeler Wilcox offers both wit and wisdom on what we might expect from a new year.

What can be said in New Year rhymes,
That's not been said a thousand times?

The new years come, the old years go,
We know we dream, we dream we know.

We rise up laughing with the light,
We lie down weeping with the night.

We hug the world until it stings,
We curse it then and sigh for wings.

We live, we love, we woo, we wed,
We wreathe our prides, we sheet our dead.

We laugh, we weep, we hope, we fear,
And that's the burden of a year.

Charles Causley

28 and 29 December are known, by the Catholic Church and the Greek Orthodox Church respectively, as the Day of the Innocents. This marks the Biblical story in which King Herod, having been warned that a child had been born who was the future king, ordered the slaughter of all the male children in Bethlehem. This poem by Charles Causley creates a frightening picture of these events, with the intricate descriptions of the 'smiling stranger' creating a sinister atmosphere, before he is revealed in the final verse to be Herod himself.

Who's that knocking on the window,
Who's that standing at the door,
What are all those presents
Laying on the kitchen floor?

Who is the smiling stranger
With hair as white as gin,
What is he doing with the children
And who could have let him in?

Why has he rubies on his fingers,
A cold, cold crown on his head,
Why, when he caws his carol,
Does the salty snow run red?

Why does he ferry my fireside
As a spider on a thread,
His fingers made of fuses
And his tongue of gingerbread?

Why does the world before him
Melt in a million suns,
Why do his yellow, yearning eyes
Burn like saffron buns?

Watch where he comes walking
Out of the Christmas flame,
Dancing, double-talking:

Herod is his name.

30 December · *from* The Tempest · William Shakespeare

The theme of this extract from *The Tempest*, a speech given by the magician Prospero, is endings. The actors of the play disappear 'into thin air' – a phrase which was first coined by Shakespeare here. This passage would have especially resonated with an Elizabethan audience, as the 'great globe itself' is a neat pun on the Globe theatre, where Shakespeare's plays were performed.

Our revels now are ended. These our actors,
As I foretold you, were all spirits and
Are melted into air, into thin air;
And, like the baseless fabric of this vision,
The cloud-capp'd towers, the gorgeous palaces,
The solemn temples, the great globe itself,
Yea, all which it inherit, shall dissolve
And, like this insubstantial pageant faded,
Leave not a rack behind. We are such stuff
As dreams are made on, and our little life
Is rounded with a sleep. Sir, I am vex'd;
Bear with my weakness; my old brain is troubled:
Be not disturb'd with my infirmity:
If you be pleased, retire into my cell
And there repose: a turn or two I'll walk,
To still my beating mind.

☾ 30 December · Crossing the Bar · Alfred, Lord Tennyson

In this beautiful poem the speaker describes himself setting sail in the evening – an image which is a metaphor for passing from life into death. The term 'bar' here means a bank of sand or pebbles across a harbour – an obstacle that must be traversed in order to sail into the ocean. The poem is filled with imagery connected to endings, such as the evening star and bell, twilight and farewells. Shortly before he died, Tennyson asked that 'Crossing the Bar' be placed at the end of every anthology of his poetical works.

Sunset and evening star,
    And one clear call for me!
And may there be no moaning of the bar,
    When I put out to sea,

But such a tide as moving seems asleep,
    Too full for sound and foam,
When that which drew from out the boundless deep
    Turns again home.

Twilight and evening bell,
    And after that the dark!
And may there be no sadness of farewell,
    When I embark;

For tho' from out our bourne of Time and Place
    The flood may bear me far,
I hope to see my Pilot face to face
    When I have crost the bar.

111

31 December · Ring Out, Wild Bells (*from* In Memoriam) · Alfred, Lord Tennyson

New Year's Eve is a time for parties and festivities, singing and dancing, reflections on the past and resolutions for the future. On the threshold of the new year, it is a time to ring the bells of change, and to celebrate the life we have. This poem deals with the loss of one of Tennyson's dear friends, but here, in this climactic moment, he stands resolved to leave the darkness of the world behind him, and instead face the light of the future. In this moment, the bells ring with hope. A happy new year to you.

> Ring out, wild bells, to the wild sky,
>   The flying cloud, the frosty light:
>   The year is dying in the night;
> Ring out, wild bells, and let him die.
>
> Ring out the old, ring in the new,
>   Ring, happy bells, across the snow:
>   The year is going, let him go;
> Ring out the false, ring in the true.
>
> Ring out the grief that saps the mind
>   For those that here we see no more;
>   Ring out the feud of rich and poor,
> Ring in redress to all mankind.

Ring out a slowly dying cause,
  And ancient forms of party strife;
  Ring in the nobler modes of life,
With sweeter manners, purer laws.

Ring out the want, the care, the sin,
  The faithless coldness of the times;
  Ring out, ring out my mournful rhymes
But ring the fuller minstrel in.

Ring out false pride in place and blood,
  The civic slander and the spite;
  Ring in the love of truth and right,
Ring in the common love of good.

Ring out old shapes of foul disease;
  Ring out the narrowing lust of gold;
  Ring out the thousand wars of old,
Ring in the thousand years of peace.

Ring in the valiant man and free,
  The larger heart, the kindlier hand;
  Ring out the darkness of the land,
Ring in the Christ that is to be.

In terms of its lyrics, there seems to be no reason why the popular setting of Robert Burns's poem 'Auld Lang Syne' should not be sung on any night of the year, but some time soon after its publication the song became associated with Hogmanay, the Scottish term for the final day of the year, and it has remained so ever since. The title of the poem is a Lallans, or Lowland Scots phrase meaning 'old long since' or 'days gone by', and the poem is a straightforward celebration of passing time with good company and raising a toast to fond and shared memories.

> Should auld acquaintance be forgot,
>   And never brought to mind?
> Should auld acquaintance be forgot,
>   And auld lang syne!
>
>   For auld lang syne, my dear,
>   For auld lang syne.
>   We'll tak a cup o' kindness yet,
>   For auld lang syne.
>
> And surely ye'll be your pint stowp!
>   And surely I'll be mine!
> And we'll tak a cup o' kindness yet,
>   For auld lang syne.

We twa hae run about the braes,
    And pou'd the gowans fine;
But we've wander'd mony a weary fit,
    Sin' auld lang syne.

We twa hae paidl'd in the burn,
    Frae morning sun till dine;
But seas between us braid hae roar'd
    Sin' auld lang syne.

And there's a hand, my trusty fere!
    And gie's a hand o' thine!
And we'll tak a right gude-willie waught,
    For auld lang syne.

    For auld lang syne, my dear,
    For auld lang syne.
    We'll tak a cup o' kindness yet,
    For auld lang syne.

January

1 January · New Every Morning ·
Susan Coolidge

January takes its name from the Roman two-headed god Janus, who had one head looking back to the outgoing year and one facing the year ahead. Here, the American writer of *What Katy Did* reflects on new beginnings.

> Every day is a fresh beginning,
> Listen my soul to the glad refrain.
> And, spite of old sorrows
> And older sinning,
> Troubles forecasted
> And possible pain,
> Take heart with the day and begin again.

117

☾ 1 January ✷ Promise · Jackie Kay

Beginning a new year is like opening a new book on to its very first page. Jackie Kay is the current Scots Makar, or Scottish Poet Laureate, and her poem is a toast to all of us at the start of the year.

Remember, the time of year
when the future appears
like a blank sheet of paper
a clean calendar, a new chance.
On thick white snow

you vow fresh footprints
then watch them go
with the wind's hearty gust.
Fill your glass. Here's tae us. Promises
made to be broken, made to last.

✹ 2 January • Infant Joy • William Blake

William Blake was a poet, painter, and engraver. Here is one of his short poems from his celebrated collection *Songs of Innocence and Experience*. It is a simple song of newborn joy – a fitting start to the year, which is itself only two days old.

> 'I have no name:
> 'I am but two days old.'
> What shall I call thee?
> 'I happy am,
> 'Joy is my name.'
> Sweet joy befall thee!
>
> Pretty joy!
> Sweet joy but two days old,
> Sweet joy I call thee:
> Thou dost smile,
> I sing the while,
> Sweet joy befall thee!

☾ 2 January · The Loch Ness Monster's Song · Edwin Morgan

2 January is a public holiday in Scotland. Edwin Morgan's poem celebrates Scotland's legendary monster in an unusual way. Composed of huge strings of wild sounds, this poem seems to make no sense at all — but when you think about it, there really is no reason that Nessie would speak any language that we could understand.

Sssnnnwhufffll?
Hnwhuffl hhnnwfl hnfl hfl?
Gdroblboblhobngbl gbl gl g g g g glbgl.
Drublhaflablhaflubhafgabhaflhafl fl fl –
gm grawwwww grf grawf awfgm graw gm.
Hovoplodok – doplodovok – plovodokot-
doplodokosh?
Splgraw fok fok splgrafhatchgabrlgabrl fok splfok!
Zgra kra gka fok!
Grof grawff gahf?
Gombl mbl bl –
blm plm,
blm plm,
blm plm,
blp.

3 January · Poem for a New Year · Matt Goodfellow

As it gets under way, there can be a mounting sense of anticipation about what the year ahead might hold – about what will stay the same and what might be completely different or unexpected or wonderful. Matt Goodfellow's poem captures that sense of excitement and uncertainty – of 'something' – through a rush of rural images.

Something's moving in,
I hear the weather in the wind,
sense the tension of a sheep-field
and the pilgrimage of fins.

Something's not the same,
I taste the sap and feel the grain,
hear the rolling of the rowan
ringing, singing in a change.

Something's set to start,
there's meadow-music in the dark
and the clouds that shroud the mountain
slowly, softly start to part.

Sara Coleridge was a writer like her father, the Romantic poet Samuel Taylor Coleridge. In this poem she uses rhyming couplets to guide us through the coming year.

> January brings the snow,
> Makes our feet and fingers glow.
>
> February brings the rain,
> Thaws the frozen lake again.
>
> March brings breezes, loud and shrill,
> To stir the dancing daffodil.
>
> April brings the primrose sweet,
> Scatters daisies at our feet.
>
> May brings flocks of pretty lambs
> Skipping by their fleecy dams.
>
> June brings tulips, lilies, roses,
> Fills the children's hands with posies.
>
> Hot July brings cooling showers,
> Apricots and gillyflowers.
>
> August brings the sheaves of corn,
> Then the harvest home is borne.
>
> Warm September brings the fruit;
> Sportsmen then begin to shoot.

Fresh October brings the pheasant;
Then to gather nuts is pleasant.

Dull November brings the blast;
Then the leaves are whirling fast.

Chill December brings the sleet,
Blazing fire, and Christmas treat.

4 January • Lines Written by a Bear of Very Little Brain • A. A. Milne

In Chapter Seven of A. A. Milne's 1926 classic children's novel *Winnie-the-Pooh*, the eponymous Pooh recites a poem that he has composed to his friends Kanga, Rabbit and Roo. It contains just short words: as Pooh explains, 'I am a Bear of Very Little Brain, and long words bother me.' The poem ends abruptly when Kanga interrupts Pooh's train of thought.

On Monday, when the sun is hot
I wonder to myself a lot:
'Now is it true, or is it not,
That what is which and which is what?'

On Tuesday, when it hails and snows
The feeling on me grows and grows
That hardly anybody knows
If those are these or these are those.

On Wednesday, when the sky is blue,
And I have nothing else to do,
I sometimes wonder if it's true
That who is what and what is who.

On Thursday, when it starts to freeze
And hoar-frost twinkles on the trees,
How very readily one sees
That these are whose – but whose are these?

On Friday—

☾ 4 January · Stopping by Woods on a Snowy Evening · Robert Frost

Why has the speaker in this poem by Robert Frost pulled up in the middle of a snowy forest? His horse doesn't know, and seems to be worried. The speaker wants to remain here alone; to give up his cold and weary journey homewards.

Whose woods these are I think I know.
His house is in the village though;
He will not see me stopping here
To watch his woods fill up with snow.

My little horse must think it queer
To stop without a farmhouse near
Between the woods and frozen lake
The darkest evening of the year.

He gives his harness bells a shake
To ask if there is some mistake.
The only other sound's the sweep
Of easy wind and downy flake.

The woods are lovely, dark and deep,
But I have promises to keep,
And miles to go before I sleep,
And miles to go before I sleep.

Although A. A. Milne is best known as the creator of
Winnie-the-Pooh, outside of the world of the Hundred
Acre Wood, he was an accomplished poet.

> Elizabeth Ann
> Said to her Nan:
> 'Please will you tell me how God began?
> *Somebody* must have made Him. So
> Who could it be, cos I want to know?'
> And Nurse said, '*Well!*'
> And Ann said, 'Well?
> I know you know, and I wish you'd tell.'
> And Nurse took pins from her mouth, and said,
> 'Now then, darling, it's time for bed.'
>
> Elizabeth Ann
> Had a wonderful plan:
> She would run round the world till she found a
> man
> Who knew *exactly* how God began.
>
> She got up early, she dressed, and ran
> Trying to find an Important Man.
> She ran to London and knocked at the door
> Of the Lord High Doodelum's coach-and-four.
> 'Please, sir (if there's anyone in),
> However-and-ever did God begin?'
>
> The Lord High Doodelum lay in bed
> But out of the window, large and red,

126

Came the Lord High Coachman's face instead.
And the Lord High Coachman laughed and said:
'Well, what put *that* in your quaint little head?'
Elizabeth Ann went home again
And took from the ottoman Jennifer Jane.
'Jenniferjane,' said Elizabeth Ann,
'Tell me at *once* how God began.'
And Jane, who didn't much care for speaking,
Replied in her usual way by squeaking.

What did it mean? Well, to be quite candid,
I don't know, but Elizabeth Ann did.
Elizabeth Ann said softly, 'Oh!
Thank you Jennifer. Now I know.'

☾ 5 January · *from* Twelfth Night · William Shakespeare

Shakespeare's *Twelfth Night* is so named because it was originally written as a 'Twelfth Night' entertainment. The Christian holiday of Twelfth Night falls on 5 January, and marks the coming of the Feast of Epiphany. Traditionally, people would celebrate by having parties, and by playing tricks on one another. Shakespeare's play ends, as many of his comedies do, with a lively song from a comical character.

When that I was and a little tiny boy,
    With hey, ho, the wind and the rain,
A foolish thing was but a toy,
    For the rain it raineth every day.

But when I came to man's estate,
    With hey, ho, the wind and the rain,
'Gainst knaves and thieves men shut their gate,
    For the rain it raineth every day.

But when I came, alas! to wive,
    With hey, ho, the wind and the rain,
By swaggering could I never thrive,
    For the rain it raineth every day.

But when I came unto my beds,
    With hey, ho, the wind and the rain,
With toss-pots still had drunken heads,
    For the rain it raineth every day.

A great while ago the world begun,
    With hey, ho, the wind and the rain,
But that's all one, our play is done,
    And we'll strive to please you every day.

6 January · The Three Kings · Henry Wadsworth Longfellow

After Twelfth Night comes Epiphany itself, celebrated on 6 January as the date, twelve days after Christmas, when the Three Kings followed a star to Bethlehem to meet the baby Christ. Longfellow's poem tells of the journey of the three wise men: Melchior, Gaspar and Balthasar.

Three Kings came riding from far away,
    Melchior and Gaspar and Baltasar;
Three Wise Men out of the East were they,
And they travelled by night and they slept by day,
    For their guide was a beautiful, wonderful star.

The star was so beautiful, large and clear,
    That all the other stars of the sky
Became a white mist in the atmosphere.
And by this they knew that the coming was near
    Of the Prince foretold in the prophecy.

Three caskets they bore on their saddle-bows,
    Three caskets of gold with golden keys;
Their robes were of crimson silk with rows
Of bells and pomegranates and furbelows,
    Their turbans like blossoming almond-trees.

And so the Three Kings rode into the West,
    Through the dusk of the night, over hill and dells,
And sometimes they nodded with beard on breast,
And sometimes talked, as they paused to rest,
    With the people they met at the wayside wells.

'Of the child that is born,' said Baltasar,
    'Good people, I pray you, tell us the news;
For we in the East have seen his star,
And have ridden fast, and have ridden far,
    To find and worship the King of the Jews.'

And the people answered, 'You ask in vain;
    We know of no king but Herod the Great!'
They thought the Wise Men were men insane,
As they spurred their horses across the plain,
    Like riders in haste, who cannot wait.

And when they came to Jerusalem,
    Herod the Great, who had heard this thing,
Sent for the Wise Men and questioned them;
And said, 'Go down unto Bethlehem,
    And bring me tidings of this new king.'

So they rode away; and the star stood still,
    The only one in the grey of morn;
Yes, it stopped, it stood still of its own free will,
Right over Bethlehem on the hill,
    The city of David where Christ was born.

And the Three Kings rode through the gate and the
        guard,
    Through the silent street, till their horses turned
And neighed as they entered the great inn-yard;
But the windows were closed, and the doors were
        barred,
    And only a light in the stable burned.

And cradled there in the scented hay,
    In the air made sweet by the breath of kine,
The little child in the manger lay,
The Child, that would be King one day
    Of a kingdom not human but divine.

His mother, Mary of Nazareth,
    Sat watching beside his place of rest,
Watching the even flow of his breath,
For the joy of life and the terror of death
    Were mingled together in her breast.

They laid their offerings at his feet:
    The gold was their tribute to a King,
The frankincense, with its odour sweet,
Was for the Priest, the Paraclete,
    The myrrh for the body's burying.

And the mother wondered and bowed her head,
    And sat as still as a statue of stone;
Her heart was troubled yet comforted,
Remembering what the Angel had said
    Of an endless reign and of David's throne.

Then the Kings rode out of the city gate,
    With a clatter of hoofs in proud array;
But they went not back to Herod the Great,
For they knew his malice and feared his hate,
    And returned to their homes by another way.

6 January · Journey of the Magi · T. S. Eliot

In Eliot's masterful poem on the Epiphany, the wise men are referred to as 'Magi' – a word that means magicians in ancient Greek. Eliot tells the story from the perspective of the Magi, emphasizing the difficulty of their journey and their feeling of alienation when presented with the birth of Christ – and an entire new faith.

'A cold coming we had of it,
Just the worst time of the year
For a journey, and such a long journey:
The ways deep and the weather sharp,
The very dead of winter.'
And the camels galled, sore-footed, refractory,
Lying down in the melting snow.
There were times we regretted
The summer palaces on slopes, the terraces,
And the silken girls bringing sherbet.
Then the camel men cursing and grumbling
and running away, and wanting their liquor and
    women,
And the night-fires going out, and the lack of shelters,
And the cities hostile and the towns unfriendly
And the villages dirty and charging high prices:
A hard time we had of it.
At the end we preferred to travel all night,
Sleeping in snatches,
With the voices singing in our ears, saying
That this was all folly.

133

Then at dawn we came down to a temperate valley,
Wet, below the snow line, smelling of vegetation,
With a running stream and a water-mill beating the
    darkness,
And three trees on the low sky.
And an old white horse galloped away in the meadow.
Then we came to a tavern with vine-leaves over the
    lintel,
Six hands at an open door dicing for pieces of silver,
And feet kicking the empty wine-skins.
But there was no information, and so we continued
And arriving at evening, not a moment too soon
Finding the place; it was (you may say) satisfactory.

All this was a long time ago, I remember,
And I would do it again, but set down
This set down
This: were we led all that way for
Birth or Death? There was a Birth, certainly,
We had evidence and no doubt. I had seen birth and
    death,
But had thought they were different; this Birth was
Hard and bitter agony for us, like Death, our death.
We returned to our places, these Kingdoms,
But no longer at ease here, in the old dispensation,
With an alien people clutching their gods.
I should be glad of another death.

7 January • Dawn • Ella Wheeler Wilcox

Ella Wheeler Wilcox's poem 'Dawn' casts day and night as lovers, and it is a perfect reflection on the theme of this book – a poem for every day and night of the season.

> Day's fondest moments are at dawn,
> Refreshed by his long sleep, the Light
> Kisses the languid lips of Night
> Ere she can rise and hasten on.
> All glowing from his dreamless rest
> He holds her closely to his breast,
> And sees her dusky eyes grow dim,
> Till, lo! she dies for love of him.

☾ **7 January** • Saint Distaff's Day, or The Morrow After Twelfth Day • Robert Herrick

This poem by Robert Herrick describes an old tradition, where men and women used to take the opportunity of 'St Distaff's Day' to play pranks on one another.

> Partly work, and partly play
> Ye must, on Saint Distaff's day:
> From the plough soon free your team;
> Then come home, and fodder them:
> If the maids a-spinning go;
> Burn the flax, and fire the tow,
> Scorch their plackets, but beware
> That ye singe no maiden hair:
> Bring in pails of water, then,
> Let the maids bewash the men:
> Give Saint Distaff all the right,
> Then bid Christmas sport good-night;
> And, next morrow, everyone
> To his own vocation.

Charlotte was the eldest of the three Brontë sisters, and the author of several novels, including *Jane Eyre*. In 1846 Charlotte and her sisters Emily and Anne published a volume of poetry under names that might be mistaken for men's: Currer, Ellis and Acton Bell. Charlotte wrote few poems in her life, but those that remain are filled with powerful expressions of emotion and deep thinking about love, friendship and life itself.

Life, believe, is not a dream
So dark as sages say;
Oft a little morning rain
Foretells a pleasant day.
Sometimes there are clouds of gloom,
But these are transient all;
If the shower will make the roses bloom,
O why lament its fall?
Rapidly, merrily,
Life's sunny hours flit by,
Gratefully, cheerily
Enjoy them as they fly!
What though Death at times steps in,
And calls our Best away?
What though sorrow seems to win,
O'er hope, a heavy sway?
Yet Hope again elastic springs,
Unconquered, though she fell;
Still buoyant are her golden wings,
Still strong to bear us well.
Manfully, fearlessly,

The day of trial bear,
For gloriously, victoriously,
Can courage quell despair!

☾ 8 January · The more it SNOWS · A. A. Milne

The idea for this poem came to Winnie the Pooh while
he was waiting in a snowstorm for Piglet to answer his
knock at the door. Jumping up and down in the cold,
Pooh found that a 'hum' came into his head: 'a Good
Hum, such as is Hummed Hopefully to Others.'

> The more it snows
>   (Tiddely-pom)
> The more it goes
>   (Tiddely-pom)
> The more it goes
>   (Tiddely-pom)
>   On snowing.
>
> And nobody knows
>   (Tiddely-pom)
> How cold my toes
>   (Tiddely-pom)
> How cold my toes
>   (Tiddely-pom)
>   Are growing.

139

Born in Wales in 1593, the priest George Herbert was among the foremost poets of his day, and many of his poems mix religious imagery with inventive storytelling. In 'The Pulley' Herbert narrates the story of God creating humans. God gives all of his gifts to man except one: rest. We have to be like a pulley: sending love up to God, and not just pulling it down to earth.

When God at first made man,
Having a glass of blessings standing by,
'Let us,' said He, 'pour on him all we can:
Let the world's riches, which dispersèd lie,
　　Contract into a span.'

So Strength first made a way;
Then Beauty flowed, then Wisdom, Honour, Pleasure:
When almost all was out, God made a stay,
Perceiving that, alone of all His treasure,
　　Rest in the bottom lay.

'For if I should,' said He,
'Bestow this jewel also on my creature,
He would adore my gifts instead of me,
And rest in Nature, not the God of Nature:
　　So both should losers be.

'Yet let him keep the rest,
But keep them with repining restlessness:
Let him be rich and weary, that at least,
If goodness lead him not, yet weariness
　　May toss him to my breast.'

The magic of Jonjo, perhaps, is that it doesn't matter whether he is real or not: the important thing is how wonderful the outside world can be.

Nobody knows what Jonjo knows. Nobody knows but he.
So Jonjo took me for a walk and showed his world to me.

I met him by the garden gate when the sun broke fresh
    and new.
Jonjo knows that fairies sleep on cobwebs laced with dew.

We strolled along the river's edge. It glistened in the light.
Sailing on a leafy boat, we saw a water sprite.

I followed him to forests and sank down to my knees.
Jonjo knows that wood elves meet in the hollow of old
    trees.

We climbed an icy mountain. Clouds drifted past our eyes.
There we spotted unicorns play chase across the skies.

I joined him at the ocean, where the mist rolled slowly
    in.
Jonjo knows a silver splash is the glimpse of a
    mermaid's fin.

He brought me to a stone cave as the sun began to fall,
to watch a dragon's shadow dance across the entrance
    wall.

We wandered in the starshine. An orange moon glowed
    bright.
Jonjo knows the man up there will keep us in his sight.

I got back home at midnight. He walked me to my door.
But as I turned to say goodbye, my Jonjo was no more.

Nobody knows what Jonjo knows. Nobody knows it's
    true.
So let me take you for a walk and I'll show his world to
    you.

The word 'epistolary' describes a kind of literature formed of a letter or letters – like this poem by Elizabeth Bishop. It is an ancient literary technique, appearing in the poetry of Ovid, making up some of the books of the Bible ('Epistles'), and forming the narrative framework for novels, including *Frankenstein* and *Dracula*.

In your next letter I wish you'd say
where you are going and what you are doing;
how are the plays, and after the plays
what other pleasures you're pursuing:

taking cabs in the middle of the night,
driving as if to save your soul
where the road goes round and round the park
and the meter glares like a moral owl,

and the trees look so queer and green
standing alone in big black caves
and suddenly you're in a different place
where everything seems to happen in waves,

and most of the jokes you just can't catch,
like dirty words rubbed off a slate,
and the songs are loud but somehow dim
and it gets so terribly late,
and coming out of the brownstone house
to the gray sidewalk, the watered street,
one side of the buildings rises with the sun
like a glistening field of wheat.

– Wheat, not oats, dear. I'm afraid
if it's wheat it's none of your sowing,
nevertheless I'd like to know
what you are doing and where you are going.

☾ 10 January • Baby Orang-utan • Helen Dunmore

Although January is a cold, wintry month, it is also the start of a new year – days are becoming longer, and before we know it new life will start springing from the earth. This poem is about the beginning of a life.

> Bold flare of orange –
> a struck match
> against his mother's breast
>
> he listens to her heartbeat
> going yes yes yes

11 January • Dust of Snow • Robert Frost

Robert Frost remains one of America's best loved poets, and he won more Pulitzer Prizes for poetry than anyone else – six in total. His poetry is usually carefully measured, and he prefers directness and simple, striking images to elaborate or intricate poems.

> The way a crow
> Shook down on me
> The dust of snow
> From a hemlock tree
>
> Has given my heart
> A change of mood
> And saved some part
> Of a day I had rued.

☾ **11 January** • Escape at Bedtime • Robert Louis Stevenson

Robert Louis Stevenson is now best known as the author of the adventure novel *Treasure Island*, but he was also a poet. Despite the lack of pirates and treasure maps, this poem describes an adventure, as its speaker manages to escape bedtime.

The lights from the parlour and kitchen shone out
Through the blinds and the windows and bars;
And high overhead and all moving about,
There were thousands of millions of stars.
There ne'er were such thousands of leaves on a tree,
Nor of people in church or the park,
As the crowds of the stars that looked down upon me,
And that glittered and winked in the dark.

The Dog, and the Plough, and the Hunter, and all,
And the star of the sailor, and Mars,
These shone in the sky, and the pail by the wall
Would be half full of water and stars.
They saw me at last, and they chased me with cries,
And they soon had me packed into bed;
But the glory kept shining and bright in my eyes,
And the stars going round in my head.

12 January · A Good Play ·
Robert Louis Stevenson

This poem continues with the theme of adventure. This
time, the narrator is describing 'the very best of plays'
that he had with his friend, Tom, when they built a ship
on the stairs of the house.

> We built a ship upon the stairs
> All made of the back-bedroom chairs,
> And filled it full of soft pillows
> To go a-sailing on the billows.
> We took a saw and several nails,
> And water in the nursery pails;
> And Tom said, 'Let us also take
> An apple and a slice of cake;' –
> Which was enough for Tom and me
> To go a-sailing on, till tea.
> We sailed along for days and days,
> And had the very best of plays;
> But Tom fell out and hurt his knee,
> So there was no one left but me.

Poems written for particular dates or days, or to
remember certain historical or personal events, are
called 'occasional poems'. In this poem, the occasion
isn't a great battle or a political event, but just a
bitterly cold January day – the characters in the poem
even start to argue about what counts as an occasion!
Jacqueline Woodson is a celebrated American writer,
and Barack Obama, the 44th US President, is a fan of
her work.

Ms. Marcus says that an occasional poem is a poem
written about something
important
or special
that's gonna happen
or already did.
Think of a specific occasion, she says – *and write
        about it.*

Like what?! Lamont asks.
He's all slouched down in his seat.
I don't feel like writing about no occasion.

How about your birthday? Ms. Marcus says.
*What about it? Just a birthday. Comes in June and it
        ain't*
June, Lamont says. *As a matter of fact,*
he says, *it's January and it's snowing.*

Then his voice gets real low and he says
And when it's January and all cold like this,
feels like June's a long, long ways away.

The whole class looks at Ms. Marcus.
Some of the kids are nodding.
Outside the sky looks like it's made out of metal
and the cold, cold air is rattling the windowpanes
and coming underneath them too.

I seen Lamont's coat.
It's gray and the sleeves are too short.
It's down but it looks like a lot of the feathers fell out
a long time ago.
Ms. Marcus got a nice coat.
It's down too but real puffy so
maybe when she's inside it
she can't even tell January from June.

Then write about January, Ms. Marcus says, *that's*
an occasion.
But she looks a little bit sad when she says it
Like she's sorry she ever brought the whole
occasional poem thing up.

I was gonna write about Mama's funeral
but Lamont and Ms. Marcus going back and forth
zapped all the ideas from my head.

I guess them arguing
on a Tuesday in January's an occasion
So I guess this is an occasional poem.

This poem celebrates the way the imagination – this time fed by story books – can create a whole world to play in, even in the confines of the house.

At evening when the lamp is lit,
Around the fire my parents sit;
They sit at home and talk and sing,
And do not play at anything.

Now, with my little gun, I crawl
All in the dark along the wall,
And follow round the forest track
Away behind the sofa back.

There, in the night, where none can spy,
All in my hunter's camp I lie,
And play at books that I have read
Till it is time to go to bed.

These are the hills, these are the woods,
These are my starry solitudes;
And there the river by whose brink
The roaring lions come to drink.

I see the others far away
As if in firelit camp they lay,
And I, like an Indian scout,
Around their party prowled about.

So, when my nurse comes in for me,
Home I return across the sea,
And go to bed with backward looks
At my dear land of Story Books.

13 January is St Hilary's Day, which is known as 'the
coldest day of the year'; not because it always is, but
because remarkably icy conditions mark the history
of that day. The nickname can be traced back to a
great frost in 1086, but it is the big freeze of 1205 that
cemented the day's reputation. The weather was so icy
that people held frost fairs, and even the River Thames
froze over – intrepid Londoners were able to skate on
its surface!

> It is midnight in the ice-rink
>   And all is cool and still.
> Darkness seems to hold its breath
>   Nothing moves, until
>
> Out of the kitchen, one by one,
>   The cutlery comes creeping,
> Quiet as mice to the brink of the ice
>   While all the world is sleeping.
>
> Then suddenly, a serving-spoon
>   Switches on the light,
> And the silver swoops upon the ice
>   Screaming with delight.
>
> The knives are high-speed skaters
>   Round and round they race,
> Blades hissing, sissing,
>   Whizzing at a dizzy pace.

Forks twirl like dancers
    Pirouetting on the spot.
Teaspoons (who take no chances)
    Hold hands and giggle a lot.

All night long the fun goes on
    Until the sun, their friend,
Gives the warning signal
    That all good things must end.

So they slink back to the darkness
    of the kitchen cutlery-drawer
And steel themselves to wait
    Until it's time to skate once more.

At eight the canteen ladies
    Breeze in as good as gold
To lay the tables and wonder
    Why the cutlery is so cold.

In January 1610, the Italian astronomer Galileo Galilei wrote of his discovery of the four moons of Jupiter. This was the first time someone had proved that there were objects in space that could not be seen with the naked eye, but which were visible through the use of a telescope (then a recent invention). Galileo's findings were not received well, particularly by the Catholic Church, and he was penalized for his claim that the earth revolves around the sun. He spent the last eight years of his life under house arrest. In Poe's sonnet 'To Science' the poet asks a series of questions. Does science serve to tear poetry and mythology out of life itself, and give us only 'dull realities'? In a word, does science make things more *boring*? It's important to note that the poem doesn't answer its own questions.

Science! true daughter of Old Time thou art!
  Who alterest all things with thy peering eyes.
Why preyest thou thus upon the poet's heart,
  Vulture, whose wings are dull realities?
How should he love thee? or how deem thee wise,
  Who wouldst not leave him in his wandering
To seek for treasure in the jewelled skies,
  Albeit he soared with an undaunted wing?
Hast thou not dragged Diana from her car?
  And driven the Hamadryad from the wood
To seek a shelter in some happier star?
  Hast thou not torn the Naiad from her flood,
The Elfin from the green grass, and from me
The summer dream beneath the tamarind tree?

The writer Carl Sandburg won three Pulitzer Prizes for Literature (two for his poetry and one for a biography of President Lincoln). This poem might seem simple for such a feted author, but its power stems from the way it takes an everyday object, a door, and makes it seem like something altogether more abstract and conceptual.

> An open door says, 'Come in.'
> A shut door says, 'Who are you?'
> Shadows and ghosts go through shut doors.
> If a door is shut and you want it shut,
>   why open it?
> If a door is open and you want it open,
>   why shut it?
> Doors forget but only doors know what it is
>   doors forget.

15 January · *from* I Have a Dream · Martin Luther King, Jr.

No one can say for sure what makes a poem, but it is usually accepted that poetry is about the sound as well as the sight of words, and about rhythm, the flow of lines, and the uniqueness of the words the poet chooses to use. Few people would dispute the poetic power of Dr Martin Luther King's speech known as 'I Have a Dream'. Delivered in 1963, the speech calls for the end of racism in the United States, and is considered to be a crucial moment in the American Civil Rights Movement. It was delivered a hundred years after the Emancipation Proclamation, which led the way to the abolition of slavery in the United States. In 1983 Martin Luther King Jr. Day was designated an American holiday on the third Monday in January, close to his 15 January birthday.

I say to you today, my friends . . .
I still have a dream. It is a dream
deeply rooted in the American dream.
I have a dream that one day this nation will rise up
and live out the true meaning of its creed.
We hold these truths to be self-evident
that all men are created equal.
    I have a dream
that one day on the red hills of Georgia
the sons of former slaves and the sons
of former slave-owners will be able
to sit down together at the table of brotherhood.

    I have a dream
that one day, even the state of Mississippi,
a state sweltering with the heat of injustice,
sweltering with the heat of oppression,
will be transformed into an oasis
of freedom and justice.
    I have a dream
that my four little children will one day
live in a nation where they will not
be judged by the colour of their skin
but by the content of their character.
I have a dream today!

    I have a dream
that one day down in Alabama, with its vicious
racists, with its governor having his lips
dripping with the words of interposition
and nullification, one day, right here in Alabama,
little black boys and black girls will be able
to join hands with little white boys
and white girls as sisters and brothers.
I have a dream today!

    I have a dream . . .
This is our hope.
This is the faith that I go
back to the South with . . .

159

Let freedom ring . . . !
Allow freedom to ring . . . !
from every mountainside . . .
from every peak . . .
from every village and hamlet . . .
we will be able to join hands and sing . . .
'Free at last, free at last;
thank God Almighty, we are free at last.'

The African American writer Langston Hughes was
a key figure in the Civil Rights movement and a
leading light in the Harlem Renaissance initiative that
promoted African American artists in New York in the
1920s. A friend of Dr King's, Hughes wrote this poem
in tribute to the former, and just as King discussed his
vision for a racially equal America in terms of a 'dream',
so too does Hughes depict freedom as a dream. That
reverie took on a nightmarish quality when King was
assassinated in 1968.

> To fling my arms wide
> In some place of the sun,
> To whirl and to dance
> Till the white day is done.
> Then rest at cool evening
> Beneath a tall tree
> While night comes on gently,
>   Dark like me—
> That is my dream!
>
> To fling my arms wide
> In the face of the sun,
> Dance! Whirl! Whirl!
> Till the quick day is done.
> Rest at pale evening . . .
> A tall, slim tree . . .
> Night coming tenderly
>   Black like me.

16 January · The Burial of Sir John Moore · Charles Wolfe

Charles Wolfe was a nineteenth-century Irish priest, but is better remembered for this poem on 'The Burial of Sir John Moore'. The poem was a favourite of the great poet Lord Byron, who was largely responsible for its popularity after Wolfe's death. The Battle of Corunna, in Spain, was fought between France and Britain on this day in 1806, as part of the larger Napoleonic Wars. Sir John Moore, a distinguished general who was in charge of the British forces, was fatally wounded by cannon fire at Corunna. Wolfe's words serve to commemorate Moore as a hero.

Not a drum was heard, not a funeral note,
　　As his corse to the rampart we hurried;
Not a soldier discharged his farewell shot
　　O'er the grave where our hero we buried.

We buried him darkly at dead of night,
　　The sods with our bayonets turning;
By the struggling moonbeam's misty light
　　And the lantern dimly burning.

No useless coffin enclosed his breast,
　　Nor in sheet nor in shroud we wound him,
But he lay like a warrior taking his rest
　　With his martial cloak around him.

Few and short were the prayers we said,
    And we spoke not a word of sorrow;
But we steadfastly gazed on the face that was dead,
    And we bitterly thought of the morrow.

We thought, as we hollowed his narrow bed
    And smoothed down his lonely pillow,
That the foe and the stranger would tread o'er his head,
    And we far away on the billow!

Lightly they'll talk of the spirit that's gone,
    And o'er his cold ashes upbraid him –
But little he'll reck, if they let him sleep on
    In the grave where a Briton has laid him.

But half of our heavy task was done
    When the clock struck the hour for retiring;
And we heard the distant and random gun
    That the foe was sullenly firing.

Slowly and sadly we laid him down,
    From the field of his fame fresh and gory;
We carved not a line, and we raised not a stone –
    But left him alone with his glory!

Hughes wrote many poems on the theme of racial inequality. The table here is a metaphor for the privileged place of white people in American society at the time. Yet the poem also contains a message of hope for the future, where 'the darker brother' will be acknowledged at the table and recognized as an equal part of American society.

I, too, sing America.

I am the darker brother.
They send me to eat in the kitchen
When company comes,
But I laugh,
And eat well,
And grow strong.

Tomorrow,
I'll be at the table
When company comes.
Nobody'll dare
Say to me,
'Eat in the kitchen,'
Then.

Besides,
They'll see how beautiful I am
And be ashamed—

I, too, am America.

17 January • Mother to Son •
Langston Hughes

In this poem, Hughes likens the struggle of African Americans against oppression to climbing a never-ending staircase. The Civil Rights Movement did not achieve equality overnight: rights were gained incrementally over decades and it is a struggle which is clearly not over, even now in the twenty-first century.

Well, son, I'll tell you:
Life for me ain't been no crystal stair.
It's had tacks in it,
And splinters,
And boards torn up,
And places with no carpet on the floor—
Bare.
But all the time
I'se been a-climbin' on,
And reachin' landin's,
And turnin' corners,
And sometimes goin' in the dark
Where there ain't been no light.
So, boy, don't you turn back.
Don't you set down on the steps.
'Cause you find it kinder hard.
Don't you fall now—
For I'se still goin', honey,
I'se still climbin',
And life for me ain't been no crystal stair.

165

☾ **17 January** · *from* Elegy on Captain Cook · Anna Seward

On this date in 1773, Captain James Cook, on his ship HMS *Resolution*, led the first crossing of the Antarctic Circle. Cook went on to be the first European to chart the east coast of Australia and to circumnavigate the entirety of New Zealand. Seward's poem for Cook is an elegy, meaning a poem that marks and laments a death (Cook died in 1779, a year before Seward's poem was written). In this extract, Seward asks the Nine Muses – the mythological inspiration for poets – to sing to her of Cook, and to tell her what would motivate someone to such wild and dangerous adventure.

Ye, who ere-while for Cook's illustrious brow
Pluck'd the green laurel, and the oaken bough,
Hung the gay garlands on the trophied oars,
And pour'd his fame along a thousand shores,
Strike the slow death-bell! – weave the sacred verse,
And strew the cypress o'er his honour'd hearse;
In sad procession wander round the shrine,
And weep him mortal, whom ye sung divine!
　Say first, what Power inspir'd his dauntless breast
With scorn of danger, and inglorious rest,
To quit imperial London's gorgeous domes,
Where, deck'd in thousand tints, bright Pleasure roams;
In cups of summer-ice her nectar pours,
Or twines, 'mid wint'ry snows, her roseate bowers . . .
Where Beauty moves with fascinating grace,
Calls the sweet blush to wanton o'er her face,

On each fond youth her soft artillery tries,
Aims her light smile, and rolls her frolic eyes:
What Power inspir'd his dauntless breast to brave
The scorch'd Equator, and th' Antarctic wave?

18 January · January · William Carlos Williams

When we think about poetry we usually think about carefully measured lines that end in rhymes. But not all poetry is rhymed – in fact, the majority of modern poetry is rhymeless. But there is still rhythm even without rhyme, and poets like William Carlos Williams are experts in harnessing the invisible powers of sound – found here in the image of the musical wind.

Again I reply to the triple winds
running chromatic fifths of derision
outside my window:
                                    Play louder.
You will not succeed. I am
bound more to my sentences
the more you batter at me
to follow you.
                                    And the wind,
as before, fingers perfectly
its derisive music.

C 18 January • Caged Bird • Maya Angelou

Like Langston Hughes, Maya Angelou was a prominent figure in the American Civil Rights movement. Here Angelou uses the metaphor of a caged bird to explore the oppression suffered by African-American citizens. The poem ends with a message of hope, however, that one day the bird will experience freedom.

A free bird leaps
on the back of the wind
and floats downstream
till the current ends
and dips his wing
in the orange sun rays
and dares to claim the sky.

But a bird that stalks
down his narrow cage
can seldom see through
his bars of rage
his wings are clipped and
his feet are tied
so he opens his throat to sing.

169

The caged bird sings
with a fearful trill
of things unknown
but longed for still
and his tune is heard
on the distant hill
for the caged bird
sings of freedom.

The free bird thinks of another breeze
and the trade winds soft through the sighing trees
and the fat worms waiting on a dawn bright lawn
and he names the sky his own

But a caged bird stands on the grave of dreams
his shadow shouts on a nightmare scream
his wings are clipped and his feet are tied
so he opens his throat to sing.

The caged bird sings
with a fearful trill
of things unknown
but longed for still
and his tune is heard
on the distant hill
for the caged bird
sings of freedom.

19 January · I'll Tell You How the Sun Rose · Emily Dickinson

Emily Dickinson was a nineteenth-century American poet. She was an intensely private person, and published only a handful of short poems in her lifetime. After her death, her sister discovered nearly 2,000 poems hidden in her room. Many of Dickinson's poems are short meditations that reflect her individual thoughts or moods. Though there is often a sadness in her writing, this poem about the rising and setting of the sun is full of wonder at something which happens each and every day but never stops being beautiful and remarkable.

I'll tell you how the Sun rose –
A Ribbon at a time –
The Steeples swam in Amethyst –
The news like Squirrels ran.
The Hills untied their Bonnets –
The Bobolinks – begun –
Then I said softly to myself –
'That must have been the Sun!'
But how he set – I know not –
There seemed a purple stile
Which little Yellow boys and girls
Were climbing all the while –
Till when they reached the other side,
A Dominie in Gray –
Put gently up the evening Bars –
And led the flock away –

171

☾ **19 January** · To a Snowdrop ·
William Wordsworth

Snowdrops are the very first flowers to appear each year
and they bring the promise of spring to us in the midst
of winter.

Lone Flower, hemmed in with snows and white as they
But hardier far, once more I see thee bend
Thy forehead, as if fearful to offend,
Like an unbidden guest. Though day by day,
Storms, sallying from the mountain-tops, waylay
The rising sun, and on the plains descend;
Yet art thou welcome, welcome as a friend
Whose zeal outruns his promise! Blue-eyed May
Shall soon behold this border thickly set
With bright jonquils, their odours lavishing
On the soft west-wind and his frolic peers;
Nor will I then thy modest grace forget,
Chaste Snowdrop, venturous harbinger of Spring,
And pensive monitor of fleeting years!

Through reading a poem a day, we are counting the days as they pass. But what are days for, anyway? Philip Larkin's short verse is a kind of warning. If living in days is a problem, then the solution is a bad one: to die.

> What are days for?
> Days are where we live.
> They come, they wake us
> Time and time over.
> They are to be happy in:
> Where can we live but days?
>
> Ah, solving that question
> Brings the priest and the doctor
> In their long coats
> Running over the fields.

☾ 20 January · *from* The Eve of St Agnes · John Keats

'The Eve of St Agnes' was inspired by an ancient superstition surrounding 20 January. It was thought that if a young woman went to bed without eating supper, lay on her back and slept with her hands under the pillow, she would dream of her future husband.

St Agnes' Eve—Ah, bitter chill it was!
The owl, for all his feathers, was a-cold;
The hare limp'd trembling through the frozen grass,
And silent was the flock in woolly fold:
Numb were the Beadsman's fingers, while he told
His rosary, and while his frosted breath,
Like pious incense from a censer old,
Seem'd taking flight for heaven, without a death,
Past the sweet Virgin's picture, while his prayer he saith.

His prayer he saith, this patient, holy man;
Then takes his lamp, and riseth from his knees,
And back returneth, meagre, barefoot, wan,
Along the chapel aisle by slow degrees:
The sculptur'd dead, on each side, seem to freeze,
Emprison'd in black, purgatorial rails:
Knights, ladies, praying in dumb orat'ries,
He passeth by; and his weak spirit fails
To think how they may ache in icy hoods and mails.

Northward he turneth through a little door,
And scarce three steps, ere Music's golden tongue
Flatter'd to tears this aged man and poor;
But no—already had his deathbell rung;
The joys of all his life were said and sung:
His was harsh penance on St Agnes' Eve:
Another way he went, and soon among
Rough ashes sat he for his soul's reprieve,
And all night kept awake, for sinners' sake to grieve.

That ancient Beadsman heard the prelude soft;
And so it chanc'd, for many a door was wide,
From hurry to and fro. Soon, up aloft,
The silver, snarling trumpets 'gan to chide:
The level chambers, ready with their pride,
Were glowing to receive a thousand guests:
The carved angels, ever eager-eyed,
Star'd, where upon their heads the cornice rests,
With hair blown back, and wings put cross-wise on their breasts.

At length burst in the argent revelry,
With plume, tiara, and all rich array,
Numerous as shadows haunting faerily
The brain, new stuff'd, in youth, with triumphs gay
Of old romance. These let us wish away,
And turn, sole-thoughted, to one Lady there,
Whose heart had brooded, all that wintry day,
On love, and wing'd St Agnes' saintly care,
As she had heard old dames full many times declare.

They told her how, upon St Agnes' Eve,
Young virgins might have visions of delight,
And soft adorings from their loves receive
Upon the honey'd middle of the night,
If ceremonies due they did aright;
As, supperless to bed they must retire,
And couch supine their beauties, lily white;
Nor look behind, nor sideways, but require
Of Heaven with upward eyes for all that they desire.

21 January · A Colossal Glossary · Paul Muldoon

Paul Muldoon's career as a poet has included a spell as the Oxford Professor of Poetry, one of the highest honours alongside the Poet Laureateship, as well as being poetry editor at the *New Yorker* magazine. While most of his poetry is serious, this alphabetical array of strange and surprising words is a light-hearted tour of the English language.

The **aardvark**'s a kind of ant-eater, an 'earth-pig' in
    Dutch,
while **abracadabra** is a charm much

favoured by alchemists.
As for that wine-coloured gem, the **amethyst**,

A Greek would place it in his cup 'so as not to be drunk',
a thought no foul-mouthed **Anglo-Saxon** ever thunk.

Azure is the blue of lapis lazuli.
The **bandicoot** is a rat from Australasia

that likes to **browse** or graze on the tender shoots of
    rice.
A **carbon-copy**'s a replica, though only once or twice.

Yellow or green, **chartreuse** is a liqueur
distilled, as always, by monks. The **coypu**'s prized for
    its fur;

177

not so the wild dog or **dingo**.
An **eland**'s an African antelope. In medical lingo

an **epiglottis** is a tongue, an **esophagus** a gizzard.
A **glitch** would be a snag or hazard.

The **ibex** is a mountain goat; **i.e.** is short for **id est**,
in Latin 'that is'. A pain in the side

was once a **jade**, a word which
we now use of the greenish stone deemed to mend the
   stitch.

A **jennet** might be a jade, in the horse-sense.
Soldiers in **khaki** uniforms tense

when they hear the siren-song of a **klaxon**,
since it almost always represents a call to action.

A **lagoon** is a shallow lake, usually on the coast.
The nocturnal **lemur** is essentially a ghost.

A **Lilo** is a rubber raft, while a **limousine**
is a vehicle whose occupants thankfully can't be seen

since they're often types who say **moi** for 'me'
and have a penchant for drinking sparkling
   mongoose-pee.

Whipped cream is the main ingredient of **mousse**.
The **narwhal** relies on its tusk when hunting Eskimos.

Nebuchadnezzar was the king of Babylon
for whom the writing on the wall was plain

as plain can be; a **nicety** may be either a subtle
or idle distinction: as such, it's its own rebuttal.

The **oryx**, like all gazelles, is thought by lions to wallow
in self-pity. An **osier** is a type of willow.

A **pickle** is anything preserved in vinegar or brine.
As one pine opined to another pitch-pine,

'He that toucheth pitch shall be defiled';
though **pitch** more commonly refers to asphalt.

The root of **prehensile** is 'prehendere', to seize;
you may already have grasped that a **quagga** is a wild
ass.

The **rouble** and **rupee** are Russian and Indian coins.
To be **scrupulous** is to have qualms of conscience,

from 'scrupulus', a stone with a cutting edge;
the reed with a razor-sharp blade is a **sedge**.

Tamburlaine, also known as Tamerlane or Timur,
was a Mongol king whose deportment was anything but
demure,

his stock-in-trade being rapine and reprisal.
The **tapir** lives as a hermit in the rain-forests of Brazil

where it meditates on **Theology**;
'In the beginning was the Word, and the Word was Algae'.

A no less avid theologian was Thomas de **Torquemada**
whose cruel streak ran the gamut

from burning at the stake through hanging by a gaff
to the flaying of some fatted divinity calf

all in the name of Truth and Justice.
On the subject of the 'thrice-great' Hermes
    Trismegistus,

or his Lord Lieutenant, Zoroaster,
my lips are sealed. I will say this; a **trundle** is a caster.

Often mistaken for a llama or alpaca, the newly-shorn
    vicuña
spits at the thought of the Norseman or **Viking**
who stole the shirt off his back. The chief
sense of **winnow** is to fan, to separate the wheat from
    the chaff,

the sheep from the goats, good from evil.
It's hard to categorize the **xylophagan**, this wood-
    boring weevil

makes of something nothing, **zilch**;
just as a worm may contain an armada, little much,

all the meanings of all the rest
of the words in this book are buried in one, a
    treasurechest.

🌙 21 January • The Snake and the Apple • Tony Mitton

This poem plays upon a common poetic theme, the Garden of Eden. The biblical garden was the home of the first humans, Adam and Eve, until the snake tricked them into eating apples from the Tree of the Knowledge of Good and Evil. God had forbidden them to do this, and as punishment for this act of disobedience, they were thrown out of the earthly paradise.

The snake lay up in the apple tree
out of the heat of the day.
'There's nothing to fear from an apple, my dear,'
I heard him slyly say.

He curled his coils around the branch
and looked with a lidless eye.
'It's sweet, for sure, whether eaten raw
or baked in a nice hot pie.'

The snake lay up in the apple tree
out of the light of the sun.
'There's enough in the tree for you and me,
and enough for everyone.'

He licked at a rosy apple
with a smile and a slippery hiss.
'You've nothing to fear from an apple, my dear.
Just take a bite. It's bliss.'

181

☀ **22 January** • St Vincent's Day Rhyme • Anon.

22 January is the feast day of St Vincent, the patron
saint of wine-makers. In France they say that if it's
bright and sunny on January 22nd, the year will bring
more wine than water!

> Remember on St Vincent's Day,
> If that the sun his beams display,
> Be sure to mark his transient beam,
> Which through the casement sheds a gleam;
> For 'tis a token bright and clear
> Of prosperous weather all the year.

This poem by Maya Angelou explores the essence of
humanity, the thing we all have in common, no matter
how different we might seem on the surface.

> I note the obvious differences
> in the human family.
> Some of us are serious,
> some thrive on comedy.
>
> Some declare their lives are lived
> as true profundity,
> and others claim they really live
> the real reality.
>
> The variety of our skin tones
> can confuse, bemuse, delight,
> brown and pink and beige and purple,
> tan and blue and white.
>
> I've sailed upon the seven seas
> and stopped in every land,
> I've seen the wonders of the world,
> not yet one common man.
>
> I know ten thousand women
> called Jane and Mary Jane,
> but I've not seen any two
> who really were the same.

183

Mirror twins are different
although their features jibe,
and lovers think quite different thoughts
while lying side by side.

We love and lose in China,
we weep on England's moors,
and laugh and moan in Guinea,
and thrive on Spanish shores.

We seek success in Finland,
are born and die in Maine.
In minor ways we differ,
in major we're the same.

I note the obvious differences
between each sort and type,
but we are more alike, my friends,
than we are unalike.

We are more alike, my friends,
than we are unalike.

We are more alike, my friends,
than we are unalike.

This poem has an incantatory and dreamlike quality.
Farjeon takes us over the horizon and back again on a
trip of the imagination.

> Over the sounding sea,
> Off the wandering sea
> I smelt the smell of the distance
> And longed for another existence.
> Smell of pineapple, maize, and myrrh,
> Parrot-feather and monkey-fur,
>   Brown spice,
>   Blue ice,
> Fields of tobacco and tea and rice,
>
> And soundless snows,
> And snowy cotton,
> Otto of rose
> Incense in an ivory palace,
> Jungle rivers rich and rotten,
>   Slumbering valleys
>   Smouldering mountains
>   Rank morasses
>   And frozen fountains,
> Black molasses and purple wine,
> Coral and pearl and tar and brine,
> The smell of panther and polar-bear
>   And leopard-lair
>   And mermaid-hair
> Came from the four-cornered distance,
> And I longed for another existence.

A nightwatchman was a kind of police officer who
patrolled the streets at night, ringing a bell and calling
out the time, as well as keeping lookout for fires and
unruly behaviour. In this poem, Graham Denton
imagines the moon as a 'nightwatchman of the sky',
giving it the task of looking over us.

> As cloak-black clouds
> of evening drift
> across his torch-white eye,
>
> the moon begins
> his evening shift—
> nightwatchman of the sky.

24 January · A Parting Song ✳ Kei Miller

The contemporary Jamaican writer Kei Miller evokes the irradiant and azure skies of his Carribean homeland in this warm and hopeful valedictory poem. Much like in Graham Denton's poem, there's also a sense here of protection coming from above — though here it's from the daytime sun, rather than the moon.

> May your portion be blue
> May your portion be sky
> May your portion be light,
> Goodbye.
>
> And May your portion be song
> Whose notes never die
> And may the music be sweet,
> Goodbye.
>
> And may your portion be soft
> And may your portion be love
> Yes, may your portion be love
> And may your portion be soft
> And may the soft lift you high
> And may your portion be sky
> Goodbye.

24 January · Moon Child · Sue Hardy-Dawson

Sue Hardy-Dawson's moon is not a policeman but a 'moon child', who creeps across the sky and drops down 'magic beans' that explain why we have dreams during the night.

In the darkness while you sleep
across the sky, Moon Child creeps
around the galaxy of dreams
collecting magic wishing beans.

And where a child sleeps below
he drops a tiny bean to grow
on the countryside or town,
cosy cottage, sleepy farm.

Where the roads and houses meet
on tenements, city streets
in the streetlamp's soft red glow
where only magic beans will grow.

Grey savannas and dry plains
on caravans, midnight trains
under leaves of forest trees
tropical islands, out to sea.

On rowing boats, ocean liners
narrow barges, junks from China
beyond the brown river's flow
where only magic beans will grow.

In houses built on wooden stilts,
tents of canvas, hide or silk,
on shanty shacks made from clay
under thatch or grey blue slate.

On the banks of muddy creaks
high on icy mountain peaks.
Underneath the ice and snow
where only magic beans will grow.

Travelling the desert sands
jungle huts in distant lands
under rooves, beneath the stars
coming home by plane or car.

Here to stay or passing by
under the ground, way up high,
tower block and bungalow
where only magic beans will grow.

Through the night so dark and deep
across the sky Moon Child creeps
dropping magic wishing beans
to fill your head with magic dreams.

Scotland's national poet Robert Burns — best known as the author of the New Year's Eve song 'Auld Lang Syne' (see the entry for 31 December) — was born on 25 January 1759. The date now marks Burns Night, a celebration of his life and works, such as this wonderful poem, which gave us the well-known expression 'the best laid plans of mice and men' (meaning that even well-made plans go wrong). The Lowland Scots dialect in which he wrote may be tricky to follow at times, but even if the meaning is sometimes obscure, the vital energy of his verse is abundantly clear!

*On Turning Her up in her Nest with
the Plough, November 1785*

Wee, sleeket, cowran, tim'rous beastie,
O, what a panic's in thy breastie!
Thou need na start awa sae hasty,
    Wi' bickerin brattle!
I wad be laith to rin an' chase thee
    Wi' murd'ring pattle!

I'm truly sorry Man's dominion
Has broken Nature's social union,
An' justifies that ill opinion,
    Which makes thee startle,
At me, thy poor, earth-born companion,
    An' fellow-mortal!

I doubt na, whyles, but thou may thieve;
What then? poor beastie, thou maun live!
A daimen-icker in a thrave
        'S a sma' request:
I'll get a blessin wi' the lave,
        An' never miss 't!

Thy wee-bit housie, too, in ruin!
It's silly wa's the win's are strewin!
An' naething, now, to big a new ane,
        O' foggage green!
An' bleak December's winds ensuin,
        Baith snell an' keen!

Thou saw the fields laid bare an' waste,
An' weary Winter comin fast,
An' cozie here, beneath the blast,
        Thou thought to dwell,
Till crash! the cruel coulter past
        Out thro' thy cell.

That wee-bit heap o' leaves an' stibble
Has cost thee monie a weary nibble!
Now thou's turn'd out, for a' thy trouble,
        But house or hald,
To thole the Winter's sleety dribble,
        An' cranreuch cauld!

But Mousie, thou art no thy-lane,
In proving foresight may be vain:
The best laid schemes o' Mice an' Men
        Gang aft agley,
An' lea'e us nought but grief an' pain,
        For promis'd joy!

Still, thou art blest, compar'd wi' me!
The present only toucheth thee:
But Och! I backward cast my e'e,
    On prospects drear!
An' forward tho' I canna see,
    I guess an' fear!

Burns was so popular even in his own lifetime that there were fan clubs set up in his honour, and the tradition of toasting his memory started in these Burns Clubs. On this night, Scots eat haggis, drink whisky, toast the lassies and the laddies, and recite Burns's verse. This poem is one that is traditionally read out at Burns Night dinners. Here are the first and last verses in the original Scottish dialect, and below in translation!

Fair fa' your honest, sonsie face,
Great Chieftain o' the Puddin-race!
Aboon them a' ye tak your place,
 Painch, tripe, or thairm:
Weel are ye wordy of a grace
 As lang's my arm.

Ye Pow'rs wha mak mankind your care,
And dish them out their bill o' fare,
Auld Scotland wants nae skinking ware
 That jaups in luggies;
But, if ye wish her gratefu' pray'r,
 Gie her a Haggis!

All hail your honest rounded face,
Great chieftain of the pudding race;
Above them all you take your place,
 Beef, tripe, or lamb:
You're worthy of a grace
 As long as my arm.

193

You powers that make mankind your care,
And dish them out their bill of fare.
Old Scotland wants no stinking ware,
    That slops in dishes;
But if you grant her grateful prayer,
    Give her a haggis!

26 January • Ballad of the Totems •
Oodgeroo Noonuccal (Kath Walker)

Today is Australia Day, the national holiday of
Australia. It marks the 1788 arrival of British ships
on the island, and the raising of the British flag. It is
considered to be a controversial holiday by those who
see it as a celebration of the European colonization of
native people and their land. Oodgeroo Noonuccal was
an Aboriginal Australian poet and activist, and the first
Aboriginal to publish a book of poetry.

> My father was Noonuccal man and kept
>   old tribal way,
> His totem was the Carpet Snake,
>   whom none must ever slay;
> But mother was of Peewee clan,
>   and loudly she expressed
> The daring view that carpet snakes
>   were nothing but a pest.
>
> Now one lived inside with us
>   in full immunity,
> For no one dared to interfere
>   with father's stern decree;
> A mighty fellow ten feet long,
>   and as we lay in bed
> We kids could watch him round a beam
>   not far above our head.

195

Only the dog was scared of him,
    we'd hear its whines and growls,
But mother fiercely hated him
    because he took her fowls.
You should have heard her diatribes
    that flowed in angry torrents,
With words you'd never see in print,
    except in D.H. Lawrence.

'I kill that robber,' she would scream,
    fierce as a spotted cat;
'You see that bulge inside of him?
    My speckly hen make that!'
But father's loud and strict command
    made even mother quake;
I think he'd sooner kill a man
    than kill a carpet snake.

That reptile was a greedy guts,
    and as each bulge digested
He'd come down on the hunt at night,
    as appetite suggested.
We heard his stealthy slithering sound
    across the earthen floor,
While the dog gave a startled yelp
    and bolted out the door.

Then over in the chicken-yard
    hysterical fowls gave tongue,
Loud frantic squawks accompanied by
    the barking of the mung,
Until at last the racket passed,
    and then to solve the riddle,
Next morning he was back up there
    with a new bulge in his middle.

When father died we wailed and cried,
    our grief was deep and sore;
And strange to say from that sad day
    the snake was seen no more.
The wise old men explained to us:
    'It was his tribal brother,
And that is why it done a guy' –
    but some looked hard at mother.

She seemed to have a secret smile,
    her eyes were smug and wary,
She looked about as innocent as the cat
    that ate the pet canary.
We never knew, but anyhow
    (to end this tragic rhyme)
I think we all had snake for tea
    one day about that time.

197

The bush ballad — a folk poem or song that describes and champions life in the rural landscapes of the Australian bush — 'Waltzing Matilda' is so popular in Australia that it is known as the country's unofficial national anthem. It's certainly more rousing and catchy than the actual anthem, the pedestrian 'Advance Australia Fair', which was written by a Scottish composer Peter Dodds McCormick.

Oh! there once was a swagman camped in the Billabong,
  Under the shade of a Coolabah tree;
And he sang as he looked at his old billy boiling
  'Who'll come a-waltzing Matilda with me.'

Who'll come a-waltzing Matilda, my darling.
  Who'll come a-waltzing Matilda with me.
  Waltzing Matilda and leading a water-bag —
  Who'll come a-waltzing Matilda with me.

Down came a jumbuck to drink at the waterhole,
  Up jumped the swagman and grabbed him in glee;
And he sang as he stowed him away in his tucker-bag,
  'You'll come a-waltzing Matilda with me!'

Down came the Squatter a-riding his thoroughbred;
  Down came Policemen — one, two, and three.
'Whose is the jumbuck you've got in the tucker-bag?
  You'll come a-waltzing Matilda with me.'

But the swagman, he up and he jumped in the waterhole,
 Drowning himself by the Coolabah tree;
And his ghost may be heard as it sings in the Billabong
 'Who'll come a-waltzing Matilda with me?'

27 January • First They Came for the Jews • Martin Niemöller

Today is designated Holocaust Remembrance Day, a day to remember the devastating tragedies of the Second World War. Between 1941 and 1945, over six million Jewish men, women and children were murdered by Adolf Hitler's Nazi party – two-thirds of the Jewish population of Europe at that time. Other victims of the Holocaust included people with different religious or political views, disabled people, those with different sexualities, the Romani people, and many many more. Pastor Martin Niemöller's lines are a powerful reminder that we must speak up and stand up for others, and not just for ourselves – and that we must never let the horrors of the Holocaust be repeated.

First they came for the Jews
and I did not speak out –
because I was not a Jew.
Then they came for the communists
and I did not speak out –
because I was not a communist.
Then they came for the trade unionists
and I did not speak out –
because I was not a trade unionist.
Then they came for me –
and there was no one left
to speak out for me.

27 January · The Shape of Anne Frank's Soul · Louise Greig

Anne Frank, a young Jewish girl from Amsterdam, was only 15 when she died at Bergen-Belsen. Her diary, published posthumously in 1947, offers an extraordinary first-hand account of life under the Nazi occupation. Holocaust Remembrance Day commemorates the liberation of Auschwitz, the most notorious of the Nazi concentration camps, on this date in 1945.

What shape does my soul take?
Is it round, like the moon
pale and ghostly, suspended above me
or is it a dark pool at my feet
an ellipse
deep
and infinite

Or is my soul a square?
A bare room
somewhere
left behind.
Or a book lined
in velvet
only to let
rare thoughts fill it

Perhaps my soul is a shape
only fit for a soul,
a blanket, a bed,
an empty bowl
Or not a shape at all
but words on the wind's gust
earth to earth
ashes to ashes
dust to dust

28 January · Yonder See the Morning Blink · A. E. Housman

Reading a poem or two a day can become a little ritual, like brushing your teeth in the morning and evening. In Housman's witty little poem, the speaker is at the point where he wants to put a stop to all of his routines, and he asks himself why he bothers at all. (And, in case you're wondering, ten thousand mornings is the equivalent to twenty-seven years.)

Yonder see the morning blink:
    The sun is up, and up must I,
To wash and dress and eat and drink
And look at things and talk and think
    And work, and God knows why.

Oh often have I washed and dressed
    And what's to show for all my pain?
Let me lie abed and rest:
Ten thousand times I've done my best
    And all's to do again.

28 January · The Moon · Sappho, translated by Edwin Arnold

The Greek poet Sappho was born in circa 630 BCE, and enjoyed more respect and admiration for her craft in her own time than most female writers did (and do) over two millennia later. The philosopher Plato referred to her as 'The Tenth Muse' (following on from the Nine Muses from Greek mythology), and she was also labelled 'The Poetess', cementing her status alongside the greatest ancient Greek writer, Homer, who was known as 'The Poet'.

> The stars about the lovely moon
> Fade back and vanish very soon,
> When, round and full, her silver face
> Swims into sight, and lights all space.

This poem tells the tale of a knight in search of the city of Eldorado – a mythical city of gold supposedly in South America. In the sixteenth century many explorers went in search of the city, scouring Colombia, Venezuela, Brazil and other areas of the continent, often plundering and pillaging native civilisations as they went. Poe makes no explicit condemnation of their pursuit, but the poem seems to argue that endless avarice yields only frustration.

Gaily bedight,
A gallant knight,
In sunshine and in shadow,
Had journeyed long,
Singing a song,
In search of Eldorado.

But he grew old—
This knight so bold—
And o'er his heart a shadow—
Fell as he found
No spot of ground
That looked like Eldorado.

And, as his strength
Failed him at length,
He met a pilgrim shadow—
'Shadow,' said he,
'Where can it be—
This land of Eldorado?'

'Over the Mountains
  Of the Moon,
Down the Valley of the Shadow,
  Ride, boldly ride,'
  The shade replied,—
'If you seek for Eldorado!'

William Shakespeare

Romeo and Juliet is the tragic tale of two young lovers
from rival families, who fall for one another but who
lose their lives in the name of their love. In these lines,
from Act 3, Scene 2 of the play, Juliet eagerly awaits
the arrival of Romeo, whom she has recently married in
secret. Impatient to see her lover, she is wishing the sun
and the day away so that night will bring with it Romeo.

Gallop apace, you fiery-footed steeds,
Towards Phoebus' lodging. Such a waggoner
As Phaeton would whip you to the west,
And bring in cloudy night immediately.
Spread thy close curtain, love-performing night,
That runaways' eyes may wink, and Romeo
Leap to these arms, untalk'd of and unseen.
Lovers can see to do their amorous rites
By their own beauties; or, if love be blind,
It best agrees with night. Come, civil night,
Thou sober-suited matron all in black,
And learn me how to lose a winning match,
Play'd for a pair of stainless maidenhoods.
Hood my unmann'd blood, bating in my cheeks,
With thy black mantle, till strange love grown bold
Think true love acted simple modesty.
Come, night, come, Romeo, come, thou day in night,
For thou wilt lie upon the wings of night
Whiter than new snow on a raven's back.
Come, gentle night, come, loving, black-brow'd night,

Give me my Romeo; and, when I shall die,
Take him and cut him out in little stars,
And he will make the face of heaven so fine
That all the world will be in love with night
And pay no worship to the garish sun.
O, I have bought the mansion of a love,
But not possess'd it, and though I am sold,
Not yet enjoy'd. So tedious is this day
As is the night before some festival
To an impatient child that hath new robes
And may not wear them.

30 January · Rain · Spike Milligan

Have you ever wondered why rain shoots down in little thin jets rather than in some other strange shape – well, Spike Milligan has an answer for you.

There are holes in the sky.
Where the rain gets in.
But they're ever so small.
That's why the rain is thin.

Following his defeat by Oliver Cromwell in the English Civil War, Charles I was convicted of high treason. He was executed on 30 January 1649. Known as a great lover of art, and poetry, it is assumed that he wrote this poem.

Close thine eyes, and sleep secure:
Thy soul is safe, thy body pure.
He that guards thee, He that keeps,
Never slumbers, never sleeps.
A quiet conscience, in a quiet breast
Has only peace, has only rest:
The wisest and the mirth of kings
Are out of tune unless she sings.
Then close thine eyes in peace, and sleep secure,
No sleep so sweet as thine, no rest so sure.

31 January • Peas • Anon.

Here, to help offset any winter gloom you might be experiencing at the end of January, is another funny four-line poem – this time about peas.

> I eat my peas with honey,
> I've done it all my life,
> They do taste kind of funny,
> But it keeps them on the knife.

☾ 31 January · In the Quiet Night · Li Bai, translated by Vikram Seth

One of the most admired of Chinese poets, Li Bai lived
during the Tang Dynasty – a period often called the
Golden Age of China. Almost a thousand of his poems
remain. Chinese New Year, one of the most important
Chinese festivals, marks the turn of the lunar calendar.
It is celebrated on the second new moon after the
Winter Solstice, which means that it usually falls in late
January or early February.

The floor before my bed is bright:
Moonlight – like hoarfrost – in my room.
I lift my head and watch the moon.
I drop my head and think of home.

February

✸ 1 February · A Giant Firefly · Kobayashi Issa

Kobayashi Issa was a Japanese poet, living from 1763 to 1828. He was known as 'Issa', meaning 'a cup of tea' – an everyday object that captures a sense of his simple and elegant style. Issa was one of the 'Great Four' masters of the 'haiku' form. Traditionally, a haiku is composed of three lines of five, seven, and five syllables. Despite the length, the haiku form is a challenge, precisely because every word must count.

> A giant firefly:
> that way, this way, that way, this –
> and it passes by.

☾ 1 February · Days · Tony Mitton

We are already one month into the year – where did all the days go? The children's author and poet Tony Mitton asks such a question, in this poem about the change that happens between days.

Old day, gold day,
where did you go?

Over the skyline,
sinking low.
Into the arms
of the waiting night
to nestle myself
in its dark delight.

New day, blue day,
what will you bring?

Light in the sky
and a song to sing.
Sun bobs brightly
up with the dawn,
spreading warmth
as the day is born.

2 February · *from* February · John Clare

John Clare's poetry is a celebration of nature and the natural world. Clare was the son of a farm labourer in rural England, and worked as a farmhand while still a child in the early nineteenth century. There is a wild streak to his poetry, which was published in the period known as the Industrial Revolution, and he presents a vision of nature undisturbed by men or by machines.

The barking dogs, by lane and wood,
  Drive sheep a-field from foddering ground;
And echo, in her summer mood,
  Briskly mocks the cheering sound.
The flocks, as from a prison broke,
  Shake their wet fleeces in the sun,
While, following fast, a misty smoke
  Reeks from the moist grass as they run.

No more behind his master's heels
  The dog creeps on his winter-pace;
But cocks his tail, and o'er the fields
  Runs many a wild and random chase,
Following, in spite of chiding calls,
  The startled cat with harmless glee,
Scaring her up the weed-green walls,
  Or mossy mottled apple tree.

2 February · Ceremony upon Candlemas Eve · Robert Herrick

Candlemas, celebrated by Christians on 2 February, is one of the twelve Great Feasts of the church calendar, and commemorates the Presentation of Jesus at the Temple. Herrick's poem reminds the reader to take down their Christmas decorations by this date as it was a tradition that any decorations not taken down by Twelfth Night had to stay up until Candlemas.

> Down with the rosemary, and so
> Down with the bays and mistletoe;
> Down with the holly, ivy, all
> Wherewith ye dress'd the Christmas hall;
> That so the superstitious find
> Not one least branch left there behind;
> For look, how many leaves there be
> Neglected, there (maids, trust to me)
> So many goblins you shall see.
>
> As crows from morning perches fly,
>   He barks and follows them in vain;
> E'en larks will catch his nimble eye,
>   And off he starts and barks again,
> With breathless haste and blinded guess,
>   Oft following where the hare hath gone;
> Forgetting, in his joy's excess,
>   His frolic puppy-days are done!

3 February · Adventures of Isabel · Ogden Nash

Nash wrote this poem for his own daughter, Isabel, who must have been a particularly fearless child.

Isabel met an enormous bear,
Isabel, Isabel, didn't care;
The bear was hungry, the bear was ravenous,
The bear's big mouth was cruel and cavernous.
The bear said, Isabel, glad to meet you,
How do, Isabel, now I'll eat you!
Isabel, Isabel, didn't worry,
Isabel didn't scream or scurry.
She washed her hands and she straightened her hair up,
Then Isabel quietly ate the bear up.

Once in a night as black as pitch
Isabel met a wicked old witch.
The witch's face was cross and wrinkled,
The witch's gums with teeth were sprinkled.
Ho ho, Isabel! The old witch crowed,
I'll turn you into an ugly toad!
Isabel, Isabel, didn't worry,
Isabel didn't scream or scurry.
She showed no rage and she showed no rancor,
But she turned the witch into milk and drank her.

Isabel met a hideous giant,
Isabel continued self-reliant.
The giant was hairy, the giant was horrid,
He had one eye in the middle of his forehead.
Good morning, Isabel, the giant said,
I'll grind your bones to make my bread.
Isabel, Isabel, didn't worry,
Isabel didn't scream or scurry.
She nibbled the zwieback that she always fed off,
And when it was gone, she cut the giant's head off.

Isabel met a troublesome doctor,
He punched and he poked till he really shocked her.
The doctor's talk was of coughs and chills
And the doctor's satchel bulged with pills.
The doctor said unto Isabel,
Swallow this, it will make you well.
Isabel, Isabel, didn't worry,
Isabel didn't scream or scurry.
She took those pills from the pill concocter,
And Isabel calmly cured the doctor.

☾ 3 February · Cinquain Prayer, February Night · Fred Sedgwick

This poem takes the form of an American Cinquain, a short type of poem inspired by the compact Japanese haiku, with five lines and a set amount of syllables per line: two, four, six, eight and two.

On this
cold night I kneel
with thanks for catkins, pale
green under the lamplight by the
roadside.

4 February · All That Is Gold Does Not Glitter · J. R. R. Tolkien

This poem appears twice in the *The Fellowship of the Ring*, the first book of Tolkien's trilogy, *The Lord of the Rings*. It is a riddle, in which things appear out of their opposites. It describes the character of Aragorn, who is set to be king, despite seeming unkingly. Tolkien took inspiration from the popular phrase 'All that glitters is not gold'.

> All that is gold does not glitter,
>   Not all those who wander are lost;
> The old that is strong does not wither,
>   Deep roots are not reached by the frost.
> From the ashes a fire shall be woken,
>   A light from the shadows shall spring;
> Renewed shall be the blade that was broken,
>   The crownless again shall be king.

221

The repetition in this poem makes it great fun to read out loud.

There was an old lady who swallowed a fly,
I don't know why she swallowed a fly,
Perhaps she'll die.

There was an old lady who swallowed a spider,
That wriggled and jiggled and tickled inside her,
She swallowed the spider to catch the fly,
I don't know why she swallowed the fly,
Perhaps she'll die.

There was an old lady who swallowed a bird,
How absurd! to swallow a bird,
She swallowed the bird to catch the spider,
That wriggled and jiggled and tickled inside her,
She swallowed the spider to catch the fly,
I don't know why she swallowed the fly,
Perhaps she'll die.

There was an old lady who swallowed a cat,
Imagine that! to swallow a cat,
She swallowed the cat to catch the bird,
She swallowed the bird to catch the spider,
That wriggled and jiggled and tickled inside her,
She swallowed the spider to catch the fly,
I don't know why she swallowed the fly,
Perhaps she'll die.

There was an old lady who swallowed a dog,
What a hog! to swallow a dog,
She swallowed the dog to catch the cat,
She swallowed the cat to catch the bird,
She swallowed the bird to catch the spider,
That wriggled and jiggled and tickled inside her,
She swallowed the spider to catch the fly,
I don't know why she swallowed the fly,
Perhaps she'll die.

There was an old lady who swallowed a goat,
Just opened her throat! to swallow a goat,
She swallowed the goat to catch the dog,
She swallowed the dog to catch the cat,
She swallowed the cat to catch the bird,
She swallowed the bird to catch the spider,
That wriggled and jiggled and tickled inside her,
She swallowed the spider to catch the fly,
I don't know why she swallowed the fly,
Perhaps she'll die.

There was an old lady who swallowed a cow,
I don't know how she swallowed a cow!
She swallowed the cow to catch the goat,
She swallowed the goat to catch the dog,
She swallowed the dog to catch the cat,
She swallowed the cat to catch the bird,
She swallowed the bird to catch the spider,
That wriggled and jiggled and tickled inside her,
She swallowed the spider to catch the fly,
I don't know why she swallowed the fly,
Perhaps she'll die.

There was an old lady who swallowed a horse,
She's dead—of course!

223

5 February · On the Ning Nang Nong · Spike Milligan

Here is a nonsense poem from the comedian and writer Spike Milligan. Nonsense poems combine some phrases that make sense with others that do not.

On the Ning Nang Nong
Where the cows go Bong!
And the monkeys all say BOO!
There's a Nong Nang Ning
Where the trees go Ping!
And the tea pots jibber jabber joo.
On the Nong Ning Nang
All the mice go Clang
And you just can't catch 'em when they do!
So it's Ning Nang Nong
Cows go Bong!
Nong Nang Ning
Trees go Ping!
Nong Ning Nang
The mice go Clang!
What a noisy place to belong
is the Ning Nang
  Ning Nang Nong!!

☾ 5 February · Spellbound · Emily Brontë

Emily Brontë was the sister of Anne Brontë and Charlotte Brontë (whose poem 'Life' appeared in January). She is usually remembered for her tale of gothic romance *Wuthering Heights*, but Emily was also an accomplished poet. The Brontës lived on the Yorkshire moors, and the often fierce weather of that landscape appears in their writings ('wuthering' refers to howling wind).

The night is darkening round me,
The wild winds coldly blow;
But a tyrant spell has bound me
And I cannot, cannot go.

The giant trees are bending
Their bare boughs weighed with snow.
And the storm is fast descending,
And yet I cannot go.

Clouds beyond clouds above me,
Wastes beyond wastes below;
But nothing drear can move me;
I will not, cannot go.

225

☀ 6 February · A Riddle · Jonathan Swift

Jonathan Swift was one of the greatest satirists in the English language. In his writings he takes up the voices and styles of other writers and literary forms, and he exposes the inherent silliness of politics and society alike. Swift's best known work is *Gulliver's Travels*, the mock travel journal of a man who goes on fantastic adventures to lands of giants and lands where horses rule over people. In the poem below, Swift uses the traditional form of the riddle to find creative ways of thinking about . . . well, find the answer below.

From Heav'n I fall, tho' from Earth I begin,
No Lady alive can show such a Skin.
I'm bright as an Angel, and light as a Feather,
But heavy, and dark, when you squeeze me together.
Tho' candor and truth in my aspect I bear,
Yet many poor creatures I help to insnare.
Though so much of Heav'n appears in my Make,
The foulest Impressions I easily take.
My Parent and I produce one another,
The Mother the Daughter, the Daughter the Mother.

226

Answer: snow

In this poem, Spike Milligan employs personification to allow the different letters to talk to each other, and the poem is full of puns and jokes that focus on the possibilities of spelling, such as 'ill' becoming 'Jill', and also on the relationship between letters and numbers, as V can also be five in Roman numerals.

> 'Twas midnight in the schoolroom
> And every desk was shut
> When suddenly from the alphabet
> Was heard a loud 'Tut-Tut!'
>
> Said A to B, 'I don't like C;
> His manners are a lack.
> For all I ever see of C
> Is a semi-circular back!'
>
> 'I disagree,' said D to B,
> 'I've never found C so.
> From where I stand he seems to be
> An uncompleted O.'
>
> C was vexed, 'I'm much perplexed,
> You criticize my shape.
> I'm made like that, to help spell Cat
> And Cow and Cool and Cape.'

227

'He's right' said E; said F, 'Whoopee!'
Said G, ''Ip, 'Ip, 'ooray!'
'You're dropping me,' roared H to G.
'Don't do it please I pray.'

'Out of my way,' LL said to K.
'I'll make poor I look ILL.'
To stop this stunt J stood in front,
And presto! ILL was JILL.

'U know,' said V, 'that W
Is twice the age of me.
For as a Roman V is five
I'm half as young as he.'

X and Y yawned sleepily,
'Look at the time!' they said.
'Let's all get off to beddy byes.'
They did, then 'Z-z-z.'

Sara Teasdale was an American poet, writing in the early part of the twentieth century. Her skill as a poet was well recognized in her lifetime, and in 1917 she was the first person to win a Pulitzer Prize for a collection of poems *Love Songs*. Here, Teasdale describes a couple out walking through freshly fallen snow.

Crisply the bright snow whispered,
Crunching beneath our feet;
Behind us as we walked along the parkway,
Our shadows danced
Fantastic shapes in vivid blue.
Across the lake the skaters
Flew to and fro,
With sharp turns weaving
A frail invisible net.
In ecstasy the earth
Drank the silver sunlight;
In ecstasy the skaters
Drank the wine of speed;
In ecstasy we laughed
Drinking the wine of love.
Had not the music of our joy
Sounded its highest note?
But no,
For suddenly, with lifted eyes you said,
'Oh look!'
There, on the black bough of a snow-flecked
maple,
Fearless and gay as our love,

A bluejay cocked his crest!
Oh, who can tell the range of joy
Or set the bounds of beauty?

☾ **7 February** · Today I Saw a Little Worm · Spike Milligan

This poem by Spike Milligan is very short, but very funny.

> Today I saw a little worm
> Wriggling on its belly.
> Perhaps he'd like to come inside
> And see what's on the Telly.

✺ 8 February · An Unusual Cat-Poem · Wendy Cope

The poet Wendy Cope has a remarkable talent to be both very serious and very funny, as you can see in her unusual poem below. She is, of course, making a drama out of the cat being dead by writing a poem!

> My cat is dead
> But I have decided not to make a big
> tragedy out of it.

The American poet Elizabeth Bishop spent most of her childhood living with her grandparents, and this is reflected in this poem. The contrast between the new cars and the old-fashioned means of transport hints at the changes that are going to come, suggesting that as life speeds up, manners and habits might change.

My grandfather said to me
as we sat on the wagon seat,
'Be sure to remember to always
speak to everyone you meet.'

We met a stranger on foot.
My grandfather's whip tapped his hat.
'Good day, sir. Good day. A fine day.'
And I said it and bowed where I sat.
Then we overtook a boy we knew
with his big pet crow on his shoulder.
'Always offer everyone a ride;
don't forget that when you get older,'

my grandfather said. So Willy
climbed up with us, but the crow
gave a 'Caw!' and flew off. I was worried.
How would he know where to go?

But he flew a little way at a time
from fence post to fence post, ahead;
and when Willy whistled he answered.
'A fine bird,' my grandfather said,

233

'and he's well brought up. See, he answers
nicely when he's spoken to.
Man or beast, that's good manners.
Be sure that you both always do.'

When automobiles went by,
the dust hid the people's faces,
but we shouted 'Good day! Good day!
Fine day!' at the top of our voices.

When we came to Hustler Hill,
he said that the mare was tired,
so we all got down and walked,
as our good manners required.

9 February · It Was Long Ago · Eleanor Farjeon

Poems are ways of memorizing as well as memorializing events from the past. The poet Eleanor Farjeon uses this poem as an exercise in memory, thinking back as far as she possibly can across her own past.

I'll tell you, shall I, something I remember?
Something that still means a great deal to me.
It was long ago.

A dusty road in summer I remember,
A mountain, and an old house, and a tree
That stood, you know,

Behind the house. An old woman I remember
In a red shawl with a grey cat on her knee
Humming under a tree.

She seemed the oldest thing I can remember,
But then perhaps I was not more than three.
It was long ago.

I dragged on the dusty road, and I remember
How the old woman looked over the fence at me
And seemed to know

How it felt to be three, and called out, I remember
'Do you like bilberries and cream for tea?'
I went under the tree

235

And while she hummed, and the cat purred, I remember
How she filled a saucer with berries and cream for me
So long ago,

Such berries and such cream as I remember
I never had seen before, and never see
Today, you know.

And that is almost all I can remember,
The house, the mountain, the grey cat on her knee,
Her red shawl, and the tree,

And the taste of the berries, the feel of the sun I
    remember,
And the smell of everything that used to be
So long ago,

Till the heat on the road outside again I remember,
And how the long dusty road seemed to have for me
No end, you know.

That is the farthest thing I can remember.
It won't mean much to you. It does to me.
Then I grew up, you see.

9 February · The Sounds in the Evening · Eleanor Farjeon

This poem speaks of the way sounds seem to be magnified at night. Eventually, however, all the surrounding noises of night-time disappear into the dreamland of sleep.

The sounds in the evening
Go all through the house,
The click of the clock
And the pick of the mouse,
The footsteps of people
Upon the top floor,
The skirts of my mother
That brush by my door,
The crick in the boards,
And the creak of the chairs,
The fluttering murmurs
Outside on the stairs,
The ring at the bell,
The arrival of guests,
The laugh of my father
At one of his jests,
The clashing of dishes
As dinner goes in,
The babble of voices
That distance makes thin,
The mewing of cats
That seem just by my ear,
The hooting of owls

That can never seem near,
The queer little noises
That no one explains —
Till the moon through the slats
Of my window-blind rains,
And the world of my eyes
And my ears melts like steam
As I find my pillow
The world of my dream.

Colouring in is, of course, meant to be beautifully neat and precise – but, as Jan Dean shows us in this poem, sometimes it's more fun to live life a little more rebelliously!

And staying inside the lines
Is fine, but . . .
I like it when stuff leaks –
When the blue bird and the blue sky
Are just one blur of blue flying,
And the feeling of the feathers in the air
And the wind along the blade of wing
Is a long gash of smudgy colour.
I like it when the flowers and the sunshine
Puddle red and yellow into orange,
The way the hot sun on my back
Lulls me – muddles me – sleepy
In the scented garden,
Makes me part of the picture . . .
Part of the place.

☾ 10 February · I Saw a Peacock with a Fiery Tail · Anon.

This classic poem seems, at first, to be composed of nonsensical things: seas brimming with ale, and houses as big as the moon. But if you read the first half of each line along with the second half of the line above, the poem shifts into sense: the sun as big as the moon, and higher, a sturdy oak with ivy circled round. (A 'pismire', incidentally, is an old word for an ant.)

> I saw a peacock with a fiery tail
> I saw a blazing comet drop down hail
> I saw a cloud with ivy circled round
> I saw a sturdy oak creep on the ground
> I saw a pismire swallow up a whale
> I saw a raging sea brim full of ale
>
> I saw a Venice glass sixteen foot deep
> I saw a well full of men's tears that weep
> I saw their eyes all in a flame of fire
> I saw a house as big as the moon and higher
> I saw the sun even in the midst of night
> I saw the man that saw this wondrous sight.

11 February · Mix a Pancake · Christina Rossetti

Shrove Tuesday, also known as Pancake Day, is the final day before the beginning of the Christian period of Lent. 'Shrove' comes from the word 'shrive', which means 'to absolve'. For Christians, the forty days of Lent are a time of fasting and penitence in memory of Jesus's forty days in the desert – Shrove Tuesday, however, is a final day of feasting on rich, tasty food. In France it is even known as Mardi Gras – Fat Tuesday.

> Mix a pancake,
> Stir a pancake,
>   Pop it in the pan;
> Fry the pancake,
> Toss the pancake,—
>   Catch it if you can.

241

Over a hundred years after Christina Rossetti was
writing, the contemporary children's poet Celia Warren
writes about pancakes in this joyous poem about the
advent of spring.

I slept like a twig in a willow
and woke to a tickle of snow.
The blue sky was gold at the edges
where the wind had forgotten to blow.

The pansies had ice on their petals
but the sparrows had sun in their wings.
They hopped on the green and white garden
as if they were fitted with springs.

The sky was still making its mind up
what language it wanted to speak;
it was slow translating winter
in words uncertain and weak.

But nevertheless I felt bouncy,
like a schoolchild who leaps out of bed
remembering it's Saturday morning,
for Springtime had entered my head:

Today was a day to pick daisies,
to skip and to skate and to sing;
today was a day to toss pancakes
to spread with the flavour of Spring.

12 February · A Prayer for Lent ·
David Harmer

For Christians, Lent is a time for thoughtfulness and prayer.

> For all I have said
> and should not have said,
>
> For all I have done
> and should not have done,
>
> For all I have thought
> and should not have thought,
>
> I am sorry.

☾ **12 February** · Lift Every Voice and Sing · James Weldon Johnson

12 February is the birthday of Abraham Lincoln, the sixteenth President of the United States of America. Lincoln was president during America's darkest hour: the Civil War of 1861–65. He is remembered as a great leader, not least because slavery was abolished under his presidency. James Weldon Johnson, an author and civil rights activist, wrote the following lines on this day in 1900 to commemorate Lincoln on his birthday. It is often referred to as the American 'Black National Anthem'.

Lift every voice and sing,
Till earth and heaven ring,
Ring with the harmonies of Liberty;
Let our rejoicing rise
High as the list'ning skies,
Let it resound loud as the rolling sea.
Sing a song full of the faith that the dark past has taught
    us,
Sing a song full of the hope that the present has brought
    us;
Facing the rising sun of our new day begun,
Let us march on till victory is won.

Stony the road we trod,
Bitter the chast'ning rod,
Felt in the days when hope unborn had died;

Yet with a steady beat,
Have not our weary feet
Come to the place for which our fathers sighed?
We have come over a way that with tears has been
 watered.
We have come, treading our path through the blood of
 the slaughtered,
Out from the gloomy past,
Till now we stand at last
Where the white gleam of our bright star is cast.

God of our weary years,
God of our silent tears,
Thou who hast brought us thus far on the way;
Thou who hast by Thy might
Led us into the light,
Keep us forever in the path, we pray.
Lest our feet stray from the places, our God, where we
 met Thee,
Lest our hearts, drunk with the wine of the world, we
 forget Thee;
Shadowed beneath Thy hand,
May we forever stand,
True to our God,
True to our native land.

🌑 13 February · Infantry Columns · Rudyard Kipling

This poem by Rudyard Kipling is about the Second Boer
War, which the British fought in South Africa between
11 October 1899 and 31 May 1902.. The continuous
repetition of 'boots' emphasizes the sheer number of
steps the soldiers were taking.

We' re foot—slog—slog—slog—sloggin' over Africa—
Foot—foot—foot—foot—sloggin' over Africa—
(Boots—boots—boots—boots—movin' up and down again!)
   There's no discharge in the war!

Seven—six—eleven—five—nine-an'-twenty mile to-day—
Four—eleven—seventeen—thirty-two the day before—
(Boots—boots—boots—boots—movin' up and down again);
   There's no discharge in the war!

Don't—don't—don't—don't—look at what's in front of
   you.
(Boots—boots—boots—boots—movin' up an' down again);
Men—men—men—men—men go mad with watchin' 'em,
   An' there's no discharge in the war!

Try—try—try—try—to think o' something different—
Oh—my—God—keep—me from goin' lunatic!
(Boots—boots—boots—boots—movin' up an' down again!)
   There's no discharge in the war!

Count—count—count—count—the bullets in the
    bandoliers.
If—your—eyes—drop—they will get atop o' you!
(Boots—boots—boots—boots—movin' up and down
    again)—
    There's no discharge in the war!

We—can—stick—out—'unger, thirst, an' weariness,
But—not—not—not—not the chronic sight of 'em—
Boots—boots—boots—boots—movin' up an' down again,
    An' there's no discharge in the war!

'Tain't—so—bad—by—day because o' company,
But night—brings—long—strings—o' forty thousand
    million
Boots—boots—boots—boots—movin' up an' down again.
    There's no discharge in the war!

I—'ave—marched—six—weeks in 'Ell an' certify
It—is—not—fire—devils, dark, or anything,
But boots—boots—boots—boots—movin' up an' down
    again,
    An' there's no discharge in the war!

As we approach Valentine's Day, here is an extremely
beautiful love sonnet taken from Elizabeth Barrett
Browning's collection *Sonnets from the Portuguese*.

How do I love thee? Let me count the ways.
I love thee to the depth and breadth and height
My soul can reach, when feeling out of sight
For the ends of being and ideal grace.
I love thee to the level of every day's
Most quiet need, by sun and candle-light.
I love thee freely, as men strive for right;
I love thee purely, as they turn from praise.
I love thee with the passion put to use
In my old griefs, and with my childhood's faith.
I love thee with a love I seemed to lose
With my lost saints. I love thee with the breath,
Smiles, tears, of all my life; and, if God choose,
I shall but love thee better after death.

14 February · Valentine · Wendy Cope

Today is Valentine's Day, the feast day honouring the patron saint of love and marriage (and also, strangely, bee-keeping). Couples send cards to each other, go out for dinner together, buy flowers and chocolates, and, of course, write poems.

> My heart has made its mind up
> And I'm afraid it's you.
> Whatever you've got lined up,
> My heart has made its mind up
> And if you can't be signed up
> This year, next year will do.
> My heart has made its mind up
> And I'm afraid it's you.

This poem by Robert Burns is wonderfully romantic.
It is written in a Lowland Scots dialect – hence the
appearance of 'luve' instead of 'love' and 'gang' instead
of 'go'.

O my Luve's like a red, red rose,
  That's newly sprung in June:
O my Luve's like the melodie,
  That's sweetly play'd in tune.

As fair art thou, my bonnie lass,
  So deep in luve am I;
And I will luve thee still, my dear,
  Till a' the seas gang dry.

Till a' the seas gang dry, my dear,
  And the rocks melt wi' the sun;
And I will luve thee still, my dear,
  While the sands o' life shall run.

And fare-thee-weel, my only Luve!
  And fare-thee-weel, a while!
And I will come again, my Luve,
  Tho' 'twere ten thousand mile!

15 February · It's No Use ·
Sappho, translated by Mary Barnard

Sappho's works, like many ancient poems, only survive
in fragments, meaning we're only left with a tiny part
of a much bigger poem that was lost thousands of years
ago. With only a handful of words to go on, we are left
to guess at what else might be happening in the story.

It's no use

Mother dear, I
can't finish my
weaving
        You may
blame Aphrodite

soft as she is

she has almost
killed me with
love for that boy

☾ 15 February · Cœur, couronne et miroir (Heart, Crown, Mirror) · Guillaume Apollinaire

This poem is a 'calligramme' – a poem where the text is arranged into a picture that expresses the meaning of the language.

N
E
R E
R V E
E R S M C
E M E E Œ
M U
M O R
A P P
L A A
F R
L E
R U M R E N E I
U L
A

L   R   Q   M   R
ES   OIS   U   EU   ENT
                 I
T~OUR~   A   TOU~R~

R~EANAISSENT AU CŒUR DES POET~S

                 DANS

          FLETS   CE

       RE   MI

    LES   ROIR

My heart is like an   SONT   JE
  inverted flame   ME   SUIS

              COM   EN

The kings who have NON   CLOS
  died one by one   ET   VI
Are reborn in   GES   VANT
  poets' hearts   AN   ET

           LES   VRAI

In this mirror I am   NE   COM
  captured alive and true   ME
The way you imagine angels GI
And not only as a reflection MA   ON

             I

16 February · Lettuce Marry · Anon.

This funny love poem is full of playful puns, delicious declarations and a greengrocer's worth of fruit and vegetables!

Do you carrot all for me?
My heart beets for you,
With your turnip nose
And your radish face.
You are a peach.
If we cantaloupe,
Lettuce marry.
Weed make a swell pear.

The world is full of odd couples, but the title characters
of this poem are among the strangest. Of course, in
reality an owl and a pussycat would be rather more
likely to attack each other than to get married –
especially in a ceremony conducted by a turkey, and
using a ring from a pig's nose! While Lear's poem can be
described as a nonsense poem, it is also, importantly, a
love poem.

> The Owl and the Pussy-cat went to sea
>   In a beautiful pea-green boat,
> They took some honey, and plenty of money,
>   Wrapped up in a five-pound note.
> The Owl looked up to the stars above,
>   And sang to a small guitar,
> 'O lovely Pussy! O Pussy, my love,
>   What a beautiful Pussy you are,
>   You are,
>   You are!
> What a beautiful Pussy you are!'

Pussy said to the Owl, 'You elegant fowl!
  How charmingly sweet you sing!
O let us be married! too long we have tarried:
  But what shall we do for a ring?'
They sailed away, for a year and a day,
  To the land where the Bong-tree grows
And there in a wood a Piggy-wig stood
  With a ring at the end of his nose,
      His nose,
      His nose,
  With a ring at the end of his nose.

'Dear Pig, are you willing to sell for one shilling
  Your ring?' Said the Piggy, 'I will.'
So they took it away, and were married next day
  By the Turkey who lives on the hill.
They dined on mince, and slices of quince,
  Which they ate with a runcible spoon;
And hand in hand, on the edge of the sand,
  They danced by the light of the moon,
      The moon,
      The moon,
They danced by the light of the moon.

17 February · *from* The Great Lover · Rupert Brooke

Rupert Brooke is best known for the poems that describe his experiences in the First World War. Here, though, Brooke writes about the things in his life that he has loved, and his love is very inclusive – ranging from rooftops in the rain to the smell of old clothes. These are the words of a man in love with life itself.

. . . These I have loved:
White plates and cups, clean-gleaming,
Ringed with blue lines; and feathery, faery dust;
Wet roofs, beneath the lamp-light; the strong crust
Of friendly bread; and many-tasting food;
Rainbows; and the blue bitter smoke of wood;
And radiant raindrops couching in cool flowers;
And flowers themselves, that sway through sunny
    hours,
Dreaming of moths that drink them under the moon;
Then, the cool kindliness of sheets, that soon
Smooth away trouble; and the rough male kiss
Of blankets; grainy wood; live hair that is
Shining and free; blue-massing clouds; the keen
Unpassioned beauty of a great machine;
The benison of hot water; furs to touch;
The good smell of old clothes; and other such –
The comfortable smell of friendly fingers,
Hair's fragrance, and the musty reek that lingers
About dead leaves and last year's ferns . . .

Charlotte Mew

Like Rupert Brooke, Charlotte Mew is perhaps best
known for her heartbreaking poems responding to the
tragedies of the Great War. But like Brooke she also
wrote beautifully on the subject of love. This poem,
the French title of which translates as 'what good is it
to say' is a gently aching meditation on loss and aging,
hope and renewal. Knowledge of Mew's battles with
depression imbues the text with an added sense of
poignancy.

Seventeen years ago you said
Something that sounded like Good-bye;
And everybody thinks that you are dead,
But I.
   So I, as I grow stiff and cold
To this and that say Good-bye too;
And everybody sees that I am old
But you.
   And one fine morning in a sunny lane
Some boy and girl will meet and kiss and swear
That nobody can love their way again
While over there
You will have smiled, I shall have tossed your hair.

In early February 2016 talks were held, under the
United Nations in Geneva, between the Syrian
government and its opponents. The goal was to
establish peace and end the Syrian Civil War, but the
conflicts continued. Michael Leunig's poem draws on
older traditions of poetry for children (even subtly
referencing William Blake's *Songs of Innocence*), using
them to paint a sad picture of modern warfare.

There is a missile, so I've heard,
Which locks on to the smallest bird,
Finely tuned to seek and kill
A tiny chirp or gentle trill.
It's modern warfare's answer to
An ancient wisdom tried and true:
When fighting wars, you first destroy
All songs of innocence and joy.

In this thought-provoking short poem, Benjamin
Zephaniah is writing about finding heroism in the
everyday.

Heroes are funny people, dey are lost an found
Sum heroes are brainy an sum are muscle-bound
Plenty heroes die poor an are heroes after dying
Sum heroes mek yu smile when yu feel like crying
Sum heroes are made heroes as a political trick
Sum heroes are sensible an sum are very thick!
Sum heroes are not heroes cause dey do not play de
    game
A hero can be young or old and have a silly name.
Drunks an sober types alike hav heroes of dere kind
Most heroes are heroes out of sight an out of mind,
Sum heroes shine a light upon a place where
    darkness fell
Yu could be a hero soon, yes, yu can never tell.
So if yu see a hero, better treat dem wid respect
Poets an painters say heroes are a prime subject,
Most people hav heroes even though some don't
    admit
I say we're all heroes if we do our little bit.

19 February · Mary Had a Little Lamb · Sarah Josepha Hale

On 19 February 1878, Thomas Edison – a prolific American inventor responsible for developing the lightbulb and the motion-picture camera – patented the phonograph: the first device able to reproduce recorded sound. As he was a very serious man, we might assume that Edison would have chosen some very serious poetry to be the first recorded sound in history. Instead he chose this nursery rhyme.

> Mary had a little lamb,
>   Its fleece was white as snow,
> And everywhere that Mary went
>   The lamb was sure to go;
> He followed her to school one day –
>   That was against the rule,
> It made the children laugh and play
>   To see a lamb at school.
>
> And so the Teacher turned him out,
>   But still he lingered near,
> And waited patiently about,
>   Till Mary did appear.
> And then he ran to her and laid
>   His head upon her arm,
> As if he said – 'I'm not afraid –
>   You'll shield me from all harm.'

'What makes the lamb love Mary so,'
    The little children cry;
'O, Mary loves the lamb you know,'
    The Teacher did reply,
'And you each gentle animal
    In confidence may bind,
And make them follow at your call,
    If you are always kind.'

On 19 February 1672, Sir Isaac Newton published
his work on rainbows, after refracting light through
a prism. Newton first catalogued five colours, before
settling on the seven we know today – Newton thought
seven was a suitable number, as there are seven notes in
a musical scale. The Guyanese poet John Agard makes a
rainbow the occasion for some reflections on the nature
of God.

When you see
de rainbow
you know
God know
wha he doing –
One big smile
across the sky –
I tell you
God got style
the man got style

When you see
raincloud pass
and de rainbow
make a show
I tell you
is God doing
limbo
the man doing
limbo

But sometimes
you know
when I see
de rainbow
so full of glow
and curving
like she bearing a child
I does want to know
if God
ain't a woman

If that is so
the woman got style
man she got style

The Scottish poet Charles Mackay here offers a
reflection on days gone by, from the perspective of the
end of his life. Despite the bitter words he uses, his tone
is wry and witty.

> I have lived and I have loved;
> I have waked and I have slept;
> I have sung and I have danced;
> I have smiled and I have wept;
> I have won and wasted treasure;
> I have had my fill of pleasure;
> And all these things were weariness,
> And some of them were dreariness,
> And all these things, but two things,
> Were emptiness and pain:
> And Love – it was the best of them;
> And Sleep – worth all the rest of them.

☾ 20 February · Don't Be Scared · Carol Ann Duffy

Carol Ann Duffy was the UK Poet Laureate from 2009 to 2019. This poem of hers is full of metaphors for the night.

> The dark is only a blanket
> for the moon to put on her bed.
> The dark is a private cinema
> for the movie dreams in your head.
> The dark is a little black dress
> to show off the sequin stars.
> The dark is the wooden hole
> behind the strings of happy guitars.
> The dark is a jeweller's velvet cloth
> where children sleep like pearls.
> The dark is a spool of film
> to photograph boys and girls,
> so smile in your sleep in the dark.
> Don't be scared.

21 February · Work Without Hope · Samuel Taylor Coleridge

The epigraph to this poem by the great early Romantic poet reveals that it was written on this date in February in 1825. Composed by the then middle-aged Colerdige, it, like so many of his works, seeks out truths about human existence in the natural world. Here the poet compares the indefatigable vitality and purpose of animals with his relative idleness and arrives at the conclusion that physical work and cerebral idealism can only possess meaning when they are combined together.

Lines Composed 21st February 1825

All Nature seems at work. Slugs leave their lair—
The bees are stirring—birds are on the wing—
And Winter slumbering in the open air,
Wears on his smiling face a dream of Spring!
And I the while, the sole unbusy thing,
Nor honey make, nor pair, nor build, nor sing.

  Yet well I ken the banks where amaranths blow,
Have traced the fount whence streams of nectar flow.
Bloom, O ye amaranths! bloom for whom ye may,
For me ye bloom not! Glide, rich streams, away!
With lips unbrightened, wreathless brow, I stroll:
And would you learn the spells that drowse my soul?
Work without Hope draws nectar in a sieve,
And Hope without an object cannot live.

21 February · How Many Moons! ·
Graham Denton

This poem makes use of metaphor to compare the moon to different objects.

The top of a tack, the lid off a tin,
A garden path, a lop-sided grin,
A banana wrapped in a silver skin,
How many moons there are!

The sail of a boat afloat on the dark,
The tailfin of a great white shark,
A funny punctuation mark,
How many moons there are!

An elephant's trunk, a pelican's bill,
A slithery snake, a feathery quill,
A frozen lake, a fish's gill,
How many moons there are!

A spiral staircase climbing the sky,
A needle threading through Heaven's eye,
An old grey sock hung out to dry,
How many moons there are!

A butcher's knife, a jungle vine,
A baker's hat, a crooked spine,
A blade of grass, a railway line,
How many moons there are!

A furrowed brow, a stringless kite,
A harvest mouse, a swan in flight,
A farmer ploughing through the night,
How many moons there are!
A boomerang, a trouser zip,
A pocket watch, a rocket ship,
An ancient coin, an apple pip,
How many moons there are!

An ice cream scoop, a pudding spoon,
A bowl of soup, a wrinkled prune,
A ballet shoe, a silk cocoon,
How many moons there are!

A bridal gown, a wedding veil,
An icicle, a rusty nail,
A tidal wave, a squirrel's tail,
How many moons there are!

An oyster's pearl, a caveman's tool,
A skipping rope, a swimming pool,
A wriggling worm, a spinning spool,
How many moons there are!

A scythe, a sickle, a stick of chalk,
A trickle of rain, a flower stalk,
A flicker of flame, a floating cork,
How many moons there are!

A postage stamp, a bony knee,
A shepherd's crook, a cup of tea,
Just take a look and you will see
How very, very, very, very many moons there are!

22 February · The Little Mute Boy · Federico García Lorca, translated by W. S. Merwin

Lorca was a Spanish poet in the 'Surrealist' tradition, meaning his work explores strange and often dreamlike images. He was only thirty-eight when he was assassinated at the beginning of the Spanish Civil War because of his political views. This is a poem about expression, and what it means to be able to vocalize our thoughts and speak our minds. For Lorca, who was so tragically silenced, it was important that even silence itself could be displayed.

The little boy was looking for his voice.
(The king of the crickets had it.)
In a drop of water
the little boy was looking for his voice.

I do not want it for speaking with;
I will make a ring of it
so that he may wear my silence
on his little finger.

In a drop of water
the little boy was looking for his voice.

(The captive voice, far away,
put on a cricket's clothes.)

This poem describes the feeling of lying in bed, as you exist in that strange zone between being asleep and awake.

> I've had my supper,
>   And *had* my supper,
>   And HAD my supper and all;
> I've heard the story
>   Of Cinderella,
>   And how she went to the ball;
> I've cleaned my teeth,
>   And I've said my prayers,
>   And I've cleaned and said them right;
> And they've all of them been
>   And kissed me lots,
>   They've all of them said 'Good-night.'
>
> So – here I am in the dark alone,
>   There's nobody here to see;
>   I think to myself,
>   I play to myself,
>   And nobody knows what I say to myself;
> Here I am in the dark alone,
>   What is it going to be?
> I can think whatever I like to think,
> I can play whatever I like to play,
> I can laugh whatever I like to laugh,
>   There's nobody here but me.
> I'm talking to a rabbit . . .
>   I'm talking to the sun . . .

I think I am a hundred –
  I'm one.
I'm lying in a forest . . .
  I'm lying in a cave . . .
I'm talking to a Dragon . . .
  I'm BRAVE.
I'm lying on my left side . . .
  I'm lying on my right . . .
I'll play a lot to-morrow . . .
. . . .
I'll think a lot tomorrow . . .
. . . .
I'll laugh . . .
          a lot . . .
                    to-morrow . . .
          (*Heigh-ho!*)
                    Good-night.

23 February · There Is No Frigate Like a Book · Emily Dickinson

23 February 1455 is thought to be the date of the first printing of the 'Gutenberg Bible' – the earliest example of a mass-produced book, with around 180 copies printed. Today, therefore, is the birthday of the printed book in the Western world – the date that Johannes Gutenberg, the inventor of the printing press, changed the world forever. Dickinson wrote this short verse in celebration of books and of literature; in it, books are vessels that transport us to far off shores.

> There is no Frigate like a Book
> To take us Lands away,
> Nor any Coursers like a Page
> Of prancing Poetry –
> This Travel may the poorest take
> Without offence of Toll –
> How frugal is the Chariot
> That bears the Human soul.

23 February · First Fig ·
Edna St Vincent Millay

This short poem takes the commonplace phrase 'burning the candle at both ends' and turns it into something positive. Although the expression is usually intended to be a warning to people not to do too much in case they become exhausted, Millay instead chooses to admire the 'lovely light' that this way of life can bring.

> My candle burns at both ends;
>   It will not last the night;
> But ah, my foes, and oh, my friends—
>   It gives a lovely light!

273

24 February · She Was Poor, But She Was Honest · Billy Bennett

Also known as 'It's the same the whole world over', this song is an example of vintage music-hall entertainment, the telling of a melodramatic working-class tale. At its heart there is a serious point being made about injustice and inequality.

She was poor, but she was honest
Though she came from 'umble stock
And an honest heart was beating
Underneath her tattered frock

'Eedless of 'er Mother's warning
Up to London she 'ad gone
Yearning for the bright lights gleaming
'Eedless of temp-ta-shy-on

But the rich man saw her beauty
She knew not his base design
And he took her to a hotel
And bought her a small port wine

Then the rich man took 'er ridin'
Wrecker of poor women's souls
But the Devil was the chauffeur
As she rode in his Royce Rolls

In the rich man's arms she fluttered
Like a bird with a broken wing
But he loved 'er and he left 'er
Now she hasn't got no ring

It's the same the whole world over
It's the poor what gets the blame
It's the rich what gets the pleasure
Ain't it all a bloomin' shame?

Time has flown, outcast and helpless
In the street she stands and says
While the snowflakes fall around 'er
'Won't you buy my bootlaces?'

See him riding in a carriage
Past the gutter where she stands
He has made a stylish marriage
While she wrings her ringless hands

See him there at the theatre
In the front row with the best
While the girl that he has ruined
Entertains a sordid guest

See 'er on the bridge at midnight
She says 'Farewell, blighted love'
There's a scream, a splash . . . Good 'eavens!
What is she a-doing of?

So they dragged 'er from the river
Water from 'er clothes they wrung
They all thought that she was drownded
But the corpse got up and sung

It's the same the whole world over
It's the poor what gets the blame
It's the rich what gets the pleasure
Ain't it all a bloomin' shame?

24 February · The Starlight Night ·
Gerard Manley Hopkins

Hopkins was a deeply religious man, and his use of the image of Christ and his mother, the Virgin Mary, at the end of the poem illustrates how important the stars and, by extension, the natural world are to him.

Look at the stars! look, look up at the skies!
  O look at all the fire-folk sitting in the air!
  The bright boroughs, the circle-citadels there!
Down in dim woods the diamond delves! the elves'-eyes!
The grey lawns cold where gold, where quickgold lies!
  Wind-beat whitebeam! airy abeles set on a flare!
  Flake-doves sent floating forth at a farmyard scare!
Ah well! it is all a purchase, all is a prize.

Buy then! bid then! — What? — Prayer, patience, alms,
  vows.
Look, look: a May-mess, like on orchard boughs!
  Look! March-bloom, like on mealed-with-yellow
    sallows!
These are indeed the barn; withindoors house
The shocks. This piece-bright paling shuts the spouse
  Christ home, Christ and his mother and all his hallows.

As winter draws on and spring is just around the corner, the first lambs of the season are born. Larkin is known for his gloomy writing, but this poem is surprisingly optimistic: there is fairer weather on the way.

Lambs that learn to walk in snow
When their bleating clouds the air
Meet a vast unwelcome, know
Nothing but a sunless glare.
Newly stumbling to and fro
All they find, outside the fold,
Is a wretched width of cold.

As they wait beside the ewe,
Her fleeces wetly caked, there lies
Hidden round them, waiting too,
Earth's immeasurable surprise.
They could not grasp it if they knew,
What so soon will wake and grow
Utterly unlike the snow.

25 February · The Night Will Never Stay · Eleanor Farjeon

This beautiful little poem takes as its theme the impossibility of keeping the night in place.

The night will never stay,
　The night will still go by,
Though with a million stars
　You pin it to the sky,
Though you bind it with the blowing wind
　And buckle it with the moon,
The night will slip away
　Like sorrow or a tune.

26 February · The Poetry Grand National · Roger Stevens

It was on this day in Aintree in 1839 that the race that would become the Grand National was first run – it is now the horse race with the biggest prize in Europe. In Roger Stevens's poem, it is the various components of poetry itself that line up to race – adverb, adjective, simile, hyperbole. They jockey for position while performing their own meanings, but they are all finally caught up in one big metaphor.

The poems line up
They're under starter's orders
They're off

Adverb leaps gracefully over the first fence
Followed by Adjective
A sleek, palomino poem

Simile is overtaking on the outside
Like a pebble skimming the water

Half-way round the course
And Hyperbole is gaining on the leaders
Travelling at a million miles an hour

Adverb strides smoothly into first place
Haiku had good odds
But is far behind – and falls
At the last sylla-
ble

And as they flash past the winning post
The crowd is cheering

The winner is
Metaphor
Who quietly takes a bow

This poem uses the comparison of a mountain to illustrate the difficulty of expressing things in language.

> Roads around mountains
> 'cause we can't drive
> through
>
> That's Poetry
> to Me.

27 February · Love's Philosophy ·
Percy Bysshe Shelley

Percy Bysshe Shelley was a radical Romantic poet of
the early nineteenth century. He was married to Mary
Shelley, the author of *Frankenstein*, and the pair
travelled around Europe with fellow poet Lord Byron.
Shelley drowned when he was only twenty-nine, but he
produced hundreds of poems in his short life. In this
playful love poem, Shelley shows how in nature two
things often meet and become one – like rivers joining
or moonbeams falling down to touch the sea.

The fountains mingle with the river
  And the rivers with the Ocean,
The winds of Heaven mix for ever
  With a sweet emotion;
Nothing in the world is single;
  All things by a law divine
In one another's being mingle.
  Why not I with thine?

See the mountains kiss high Heaven,
  And the waves clasp one another;
No sister-flower would be forgiven
  If it disdained its brother;
And the sunlight clasps the earth,
  And the moonbeams kiss the sea:
What is all this sweet work worth
  If thou kiss not me?

283

Brian Patten came to fame as one of the Liverpool poets of the 1960s. This poem is an example of a haiku, the form which originated in Japan and then adopted by many poets writing in English. People often refer to the idea of 'the man in the moon', because from earth some of the moon's craters seem to resemble facial features.

'Turn that music down!'
Shouted the grumbly moon to
The rock 'n' roll stars.

Ford Madox Ford was a prolific novelist, writing in the early twentieth century. He was friends with many of the great writers of his day, from Joseph Conrad to Ernest Hemingway, and he was responsible for publishing many of their works in his magazine *The English Review*. 'In Tenebris' is a Latin phrase meaning 'in darkness'. The poem tells of the narrator, amid winter darkness, yearning for the coming of spring.

All within is warm,
　Here without it's very cold,
　Now the year is grown so old
And the dead leaves swarm.

In your heart is light,
　Here without it's very dark,
　When shall I hear the lark?
When see aright?

Oh, for a moment's space!
　Draw the clinging curtains wide
　Whilst I wait and yearn outside
Let the light fall on my face.

285

This wonderful short poem conveys a message of optimism about the approach of Spring.

Over the land freckled with snow half-thawed
The speculating rooks at their nests cawed
And saw from elm-tops, delicate as flower of grass,
What we below could not see, Winter pass.

29 February · My Hearts Leaps Up · William Wordsworth

Today is Leap Day – the day added to calendars every four years to make up for the fact that it takes the earth 365 ¼ days to travel around the sun. Leap years originated in 45 BC, with the birth of the 'Julian' calendar, named after the Roman emperor Julius Caesar. In Wordsworth's poem, it is his heart, and not the year, which is leaping, but the poem does talk about measuring out days. The poem is famous for the memorable line 'The Child is father of the Man', and even Wordsworth himself went on to quote it in later poems.

> My heart leaps up when I behold
>   A rainbow in the sky:
> So was it when my life began;
> So is it now I am a man;
> So be it when I shall grow old,
>   Or let me die!
> The Child is father of the Man;
> And I could wish my days to be
> Bound each to each by natural piety.

287

☾ 29 February · Soldier, Soldier, Won't You Marry Me? · Anon.

It is a tradition in Britain that women are only allowed to propose to men on leap years. This poem tells the story of a young woman deceived by a dishonest soldier, who doesn't seem to have his reasons for not being able to marry her in the correct order.

Soldier, soldier, won't you marry me
With your musket, fife and drum?
O no sweet maid, I cannot marry you
For I have no coat to put on.
So up she went to her grandfather's chest
And she got him a coat of the very, very best
And the soldier put it on.

O soldier, soldier, won't you marry me
With your musket, fife and drum?
O no sweet maid, I cannot marry you
For I have no hat to put on.
So up she went to her grandfather's chest
And she got him a hat of the very, very best
And the soldier put it on.

O soldier, soldier, won't you marry me
With your musket, fife and drum?
O no sweet maid, I cannot marry you
For I have no gloves to put on.
So up she went to her grandfather's chest
And she got him a pair of the very, very best
And the soldier put them on.

O soldier, soldier, won't you marry me
With your musket, fife and drum?
O no sweet maid, I cannot marry you
For I have no boots to put on.
So up she went to her grandfather's chest
And she got him a pair of the very, very best
And the soldier put them on.

O soldier, soldier, won't you marry me
With your musket, fife and drum?
O no sweet maid, I cannot marry you
For I have a wife of my own.

Index of First Lines

291

293

295

Index of Poets and Translators

Acknowledgements

The compiler and publisher would like to thank the following for permission to use copyright material:

Agard, John: 'Rainbow' copyright © John Agard 1983. Reproduced by kind permission of John Agard c/o Caroline Sheldon Literary Agency Ltd; **Angelou, Maya:** 'Still I Rise', 'Amazing Peace', 'Caged Bird' and 'Human Family' from *The Complete Poetry* copyright © Maya Angelou 2015. Reprinted by permission of Virago, an imprint of Little, Brown Book Group; **Auden, W. H:** 'Refugee Blues' from *Collected Auden* (Faber & Faber, 2004) copyright © W. H. Auden. Reprinted by permission of Curtis Brown Ltd; **Betjeman, John:** 'Christmas' © The Estate of John Betjeman 1955, 1958, 1960, 1962, 1964, 1966, 1970, 1979, 1981, 1982, 2001. Reproduced by permission of Hodder and Stoughton Limited; **Bevan, Clare:** 'Just Doing My Job' first published in *We Three Kings*, ed: Brian Moses, Macmillan Children's Books 1998; **Bishop, Elizabeth:** 'Letter to N.Y.', 'Manners' and 'One Art' from *Poems: The Centenery Edtion* by Elizabeth Bishop (Chatto & Windus, 2011) by permission of Penguin Random House; **Calder, Dave:** 'In The Last Quarter' by permission of the author; **Causley, Charles:** 'At Nine of the Night' from *I Had A Little cat – Collected Poems For Children* (Macmillan Children's Books), 'Innocents' Song' from *Collected Poems 1951–2000* (Macmillan) All poems published by permission of David Higham Associates on behalf of the estate of the author; **Clarke, Gillian:** The Year's Midnight' from *Selected Poems* by Gillian Clarke. Published by Picador, 2016. Copyright © Gillian Clarke. All reproduced by permission of the author c/o Rogers, Coleridge & White Ltd, 20 Powis Mews, London, W11 1JN; **Coe, Mandy:** 'Slip into Sleep' by permission of the author; **Coelho, Joseph:** 'Rosa Parks – 1st December 1955' by Joseph Coelho. Copyright © Joseph Coehlo 2017. Reproduced with kind permission of Joseph Coelho c/o Caroline Sheldon Literary Agency Ltd; **Cope, Wendy:** 'An Unusual Cat-Poem' and 'Valentine' from *Serious Concerns* (Faber & Faber, 2002) copyright © Wendy Cope 1992. Reproduced by permission of Faber & Faber Ltd. Printed by permission of United Agents www.unitedagents.co.uk on behalf of Wendy Cope; **Cotton, John:** 'A Week to Christmas' by permission of the author; **Cummings, E.E.:** 'little tree' copyright 1925, 1953, © 1991 by the Trustees for the E. E. Cummings Trust. Copyright © 1976 by George James Firmage. Used by permission of Liveright Publishing Corporation; **Dean, Jan:** 'Rosa Parks' by permission of the author, 'Colouring In' first published in *Mice on Ice*, ed: Morgan, Macmillan Children's Books 2004; **de la Mare, Walter:** 'Napoleon' by permission of The

297